MARY HOGAN

SUSANNA LOVES
LONDON

SIMON AND SCHUSTER

TO ALL THE AMAZING TEENS I MET IN LONDON,
CAMBRIDGE, AND THE COTSWOLDS.

SIMON AND SCHUSTER
First published in Great Britain in 2007
By Simon & Schuster UK Ltd
A CBS COMPANY

1 3 5 7 9 10 8 6 4 2

Simon & Schuster UK Ltd
1st Floor,
222 Gray's Inn Road,
London WC1X 8HB

A CIP catalogue record for this book is
available from the British Library.

ISBN: 978-1-41690-160-0

Set in 13/17.5 pt Adobe Garamond by
Rowland Phototypesetting Ltd, Bury St Edmunds, Suffolk
Printed and bound in Great Britain by
CPI Cox & Wyman, Reading, Berkshire RG1 8EX

ONE

First, I brush up on the lingo. *Ring* me instead of *call* me, *tube* instead of *subway*, *TV* instead of *tube*, *chips* instead of *fries*, *crisps* instead of *chips* ... I study the latest on Keira, Kylie and Kate Moss. Even though I'll be an American in London, I'd rather die than be one of *those* Americans: Hawaiian shirt, cowboy hat, big hair, loud mouth – a general 'tude that they are all that. (You know who you are.) Not my style at all. My plan is to blend in, not stick out. What better way to observe British teens in their natural habitat than by being invisible?

'Breathe,' I say out loud. Standing in my New York City bedroom, deciding what to pack, I feel my chest burn. It's been nearly impossible to breathe normally since Nell Wickham, the editor-in-chief of *Scene* magazine, looked away from her mirror long enough to smile on me. She called me *hers*. She even called me 'Susanna' instead of every imaginable mangling of my name. But, best of all, she entrusted me with a mission: fly to London and report on the local teen scene for the brand-new, aptly-titled *Teen Scene* magazine. Can you believe it? London. As in England. Where the Arctic Monkeys were born and Daniel Radcliffe read his first *Harry Potter*. The town where tabloids rock.

I, Susanna Barringer, am going international. I've already done New York, Los Angeles and the wilds of Fashion Week. Tomorrow, I take London by storm. The city on the Thames. Where James Blunt has a flat and the Queen has a palace.

Sweet!

Up to this moment in my ever-blossoming career, I've endured multiple humiliations: squeezing into tiny clothes in *Scene*'s fashion closet, riding to the Academy Awards in the trunk of a limo, getting thrown off a set, out of a theatre, exposed from behind a rack of designer duds, seeing my butt on the cover of *Scene* magazine. Now, those embarrassing days are behind me. I'm no longer the nerdy high-schooler who tripped into the internship of a lifetime. It's my time to shine. Get ready, world! Here I come – Susanna Barringer – the fearless reporter who gets the story no matter what.

Of course, I'll be flying three thousand miles into a foreign country, by myself, for an entire month. And I'll be staying with Nell's sister in a village *outside* London which may be more of a nightmare than a dream. Plus, I have no idea exactly how I'm going to get a scoop and I've never liked tea. Do they even *have* Starbucks in Europe?

What*ev*. I can handle anything that comes my way. Even tea. Or steak and kidney pie. Or a Mini-Me of Nell who makes my life a living hell. Starting tomorrow, I'll be free to do what I do best: defy the odds and show everyone what a mere Millennial can do. I very nearly have it *all*. Including (sigh) a real, live boyfriend . . .

Let me back up a few months.

Irony of ironies, my love life began in the Virgin Megastore.

'Did you see that fact-checker video on *Funny or Die*?' Ben McDermott asked me.

We were sitting in the downstairs café of the Virgin Megastore in Times Square, sharing a brownie. For the first time in my life, I couldn't even finish my half. Fashion Week was over, the school year had just begun. My stomach was doing somersaults. Ben looked unbearably cute. His reddish-brown hair was gelled, his cheeks were pink. When he smiled, the edges of his blue eyes crinkled like Christmas paper.

'Yeah,' I said. 'It was hilarious.'

My skin was on fire. Ben wasn't my boyfriend *yet*. That day in the café, we were just getting to know each other again. See, Ben McDermott was my first love – in ninth grade, when I didn't know what love was. Not that I do now. But before I could even try to figure it out, Ben moved to Chicago. Yeah, I know. Seriously bunk. Then he moved back and we ran into each other and my skin erupted in flames.

'You're so tall,' he said to me.

I was wearing the same Payless platform shoes I'm wearing now. The four-inch height shaves off a cool five pounds. Which, BTW, is how I view my body now: I'm not fat, I'm too short for my weight. Unless, of course, I'm wearing four-inch platforms. Then, I'm just right.

'I've been working on an online video with my friend, Jason,' Ben said to me that day.

'Yeah?'

'It's harder than it looks.'

'Yeah.'

'Still, it'll be totally cool when we're done. I'm

hoping to use my video to get into the film department at USC.'

'Oh yeah?'

Stop saying, yeah, *Susanna!* I screamed in my head. *What happened to the stellar vocabulary that got you two bylines in* Scene *magazine?! And did he just say USC?? As in US* California?

Ben must have sensed me freaking out, because he asked, 'Wanna roll out of here?'

'Affirmative,' I said, sounding like the doof of the century.

We stood. I wobbled in my platform shoes. Up the escalator and through the revolving door, we emerged into the neon circus of Times Square. Tourists bumped into us as we walked. I wanted to grab Ben's hand, but waited for him to grab mine. I still wasn't sure where we were heading – relationship-wise – and I wanted him to lead the way.

'Chicago is awesome,' he said. 'But I've missed New York.'

Before my brain had the chance to review what my mouth was about to say, I blurted out, 'I've missed *you.*'

Instantly, my eyes went wide and my skin went pale. I wanted to gobble up the words the moment I spat them out.

'I mean—' I spluttered. But it was too late. There, beneath the blue globe of Planet Hollywood, Ben McDermott sent me into orbit. He took my face between his two warm hands and kissed me. Right there on Broadway and Forty-Fifth.

'I've missed you, too,' he whispered. Then he kissed me harder.

'Susanna!' Mom interrupts the sweet memory of Ben's first two kisses by yelling down the hall.

'What?' I yell back through my bedroom door.

'Mel is here,' she says.

My heart plummets. Mel (Amelia) is my best friend. Ben (sigh) is my boyfriend. The boy I've kissed hundreds of times since that over-the-moon moment in Times Square. Tonight, on the night flight out of JFK airport, I'll be leaving them both behind.

TWO

'Light raincoat.'

'Check.'

'Dark sunglasses.'

'Check.'

'Cool walking shoes.'

'Check.'

I hold up my white Reebok sneakers. Amelia groans.

'Even *I* know those aren't cool walking shoes,' she says.

Mel has a point. Wearing giant white boots on my feet will instantly expose me as an American. But platform sandals? Flip-flops? How can I take the risk? It *rains* in London. Even in summer. Like New York, it's a walking town. I'm supposed to cross London Bridge with bare toes? Somehow it doesn't seem right.

'I'll upgrade when I get there,' I say. 'My job on Day One will be to scope out the British shoe situation, and use my emergency money to give my feet a stiff upper lip.'

Mel laughs. Then she falls backward on my bed.

'An entire month,' she moans. 'How will I live?'

I join her on top of my puffy white quilt. Together, we stare at the ceiling.

'You'll continue to save the world,' I reply, 'while you continue to save for Harvard. Hopefully, you'll squeeze in a few moments to email me every single day.'

'Why won't Nell give you an international cell phone?' she asks.

I laugh. 'Nell barely gave me a plane ticket. Not that I'm complaining.'

How could I complain? How many high-schoolers are allowed to spend a month alone in another country? With a paycheck, no less. Granted, it's a puny paycheck. But still, I'll be on my own in London with my own money. Maybe I'll buy *two* pairs of shoes. And a handbag to go with them. Not that your bag *has* to match your shoes. A valuable lesson I learned at Fashion Week.

My room grows quiet as Mel and I wander into our own thoughts. Then I release one of mine into the air.

'Ever feel like you're at the edge of adulthood and all it takes is one tiny tiptoe for your entire childhood to be over?'

Mel looks at me thoughtfully and nods. I'd been having sporadic deep thoughts since Nell convinced my parents that I was mature enough to handle a month on my own in Europe.

'Face it, Susanna,' she says, 'your parents never would have allowed this if you were any other girl.'

We both know what she's talking about. I, Susanna Barringer, am a very specific type of girl. A virgin. With a capital 'V'. Amelia is a virgin, too. So is Ben. Or so he says. But I believe him. His cheeks get seriously hot when we kiss, and I can feel his heart thudding. Together, we've run the bases a few times, but never hit home plate. Honestly, it just never felt right. I'm not one of those 'Abstinence Only' freaks. 'Abstinence for Now' is more my style. What's the rush? My first time will only be first once. I need to be *sure* I'm in love. Not to mention the fact that, thanks to biology, a girl can't just walk away from a mistake like a guy can. Not that Ben ever would. But he *could*. And I couldn't. So, I prefer to wait.

'Maybe you'll lose it to Prince William,' Mel jokes.

'Now *that* would be a scoop!' I say.

Still staring at the ceiling, I imagine being with Ben. He *is* totally awesome. *My* cheeks flush just thinking about him. But, is it love? *True* love? The type of love that elicits a deliberate, romantic, fireworks-inspiring home run? And, why am I using a stupid baseball analogy anyway? That's not the way I view sex at all. For me, my first time will be more like spinning through a field of sunflowers on a warm day. Feeling both exhilarated and relaxed. Tall and small. At one with Mother Nature. Ready to bloom.

'Sweetie?'

Mom pokes her head into my room. My three brothers – three-year-old triplets – shove their way in behind her.

'Melly!' Sam says, dashing over to Amelia. His mirror images – Evan and Henry – climb onto the bed with Mel and me.

'Sanna!' Henry squeals.

'The three-ring circus wants to say goodnight,' Mom says, laughing.

My mother sits at my desk and pushes her hair off her face. The Trips climb onto my bed and cuddle Mel and me.

'I'm going to miss this slobber,' I say.

'We're all going to miss you, honey,' Mom replies.

I hug each wriggling bundle and kiss them each on top of their silky blond heads. Mel kisses them, too. In their pyjamas, smelling of shampoo and soap, I'm overcome with the desire to cuddle my brothers and never let them go.

'Say, "goodnight Susanna",' Mom says.

'Say gnigh, Susanna,' Evan repeats.

I laugh. Mom stands and corrals the Trips through my open doorway.

'Book time, boys, then bedtime,' she announces, leaving me feeling suddenly weepy.

'I'm going to miss those little goofballs,' I say.

Amelia quickly rises up from my bed.

'If you run into Sir Paul McCartney,' she says, 'tell him to start dating women his own age.'

'You're leaving already?' I sniff.

'You know I can't stand goodbyes. And you're disintegrating fast.'

As always, my BFF is right. I feel the way I felt before the first day of high school. A sort of lonely excitement. I know a great adventure is ahead, yet, at this moment, I long to stop the clock and stay right where I am. In my childhood. Before one tiny tiptoe ends it all.

Mel pulls me to my feet. I hug her hard. She hugs

me back, even harder, then leaves without another word. It's our new way of saying goodbye. Never saying it at all.

THREE

August in New York City is a sweaty, stinky soup. Tonight is no exception. I smell the city through my open bedroom window. It's garbage night. The steamy air falls heavily on my skin.

'All packed?' Dad brings me an iced coffee.

'You look like you need that more than I do,' I say, while I sit on top of my suitcase in an attempt to zip it up.

My dad, the nerdy CSI, was out all day at a downtown crime scene. His hair is flat and his lips are pale. Unlike TV's crime scene investigators, Dad doesn't wear Armani suits or 'product' in his hair. And the female CSIs in his office would never wear a tight cami that revealed their cleavage. We laugh every time we see the television show, it's so unreal. Though my dad has to admit it's far more riveting than the real job. On TV, the case is solved within an hour.

'Need a second butt?' Dad asks me as I totter on top of my suitcase.

I wince at the thought.

'Can you rephrase that? Something less horrifying?'

He laughs. Dad puts the iced coffee on my dresser and helps me close my bursting suitcase. I've packed everything I own that doesn't look American. Nothing with stars or stripes. Mostly, I'm bringing the black shirts and black pants that Sasha, the fashion diva of *Scene* magazine, gave me to create what she insisted should be 'the core' of my wardrobe.

'Begin with black and pop with accessories,' she advised me.

'Even in summer?' I asked.

'Wear black cotton.'

'I look like a penguin,' I said.

'Yes, you do,' she replied, 'which is why you need to wear black.'

Any other girl would have been bruised by Sasha's remarks, which of course I was, until I tried on my new Goth wardrobe and saw that she was right. Black *is* slimming . . . particularly when worn with my four-inch platform shoes from Payless. Which I'm wearing on the plane.

'When do you expect Ben?' Dad asks. My suitcase is

finally closed and we're both panting. 'I'll need some youthful muscle to get this luggage in the car.'

Chuckling, I say, 'Save him for my carry-on bag.'

As if on cue, I hear the faint buzz of our apartment's intercom announcing that Ben is downstairs. Dad hands me my iced coffee and wipes the water mark off my dresser with the tail of his shirt. Kissing me on the forehead, he turns to leave.

'Wait a sec,' I say.

'Hmmmm?'

My eyes instantly flood with tears. A jumble of words tumbles through my brain. *Thank you for trusting me, Dad. I'm going to miss you SO much. Will you miss me? Did I say thank you? Do you know how lucky I am to have parents like you and Mom?*

'You're the best,' I splutter.

He grins and cups my chin with his warm hand.

'And I was only aiming for the top ten,' he says.

'Hey.'

Ben appears in my doorway carrying a bouquet of flowers. Long-stemmed *sun*flowers. Can you believe it? Unable to hold it in any longer, I disintegrate into a mass of snot and sobbing.

'Oh, uh—' Wide-eyed, Ben stands frozen. The sunflowers tremble in his hands. 'Are you okay?'

'Yes,' I blubber. 'I'm fine.'

Dad pats Ben on the shoulder and says, 'We leave in fifteen minutes.'

The moment he's gone, I fling my arms around Ben's neck and say, 'You're the best of the best.'

Then I cry some more. How can I be leaving my life, my best friend *and* a boy who brings me sunflowers?

The elevator is waiting. So is my mother.

'Email me the minute you get there,' she says, engulfing me in a bear hug. 'Keep your room neat in Nell's sister's house. Beware British strangers – their accent makes them sound nice. Don't be fooled. If you get into any kind of trouble, remember the police are called Bobbies or Coppers.'

'You read too much Agatha Christie, Mom. Those terms are ancient.'

'Aren't lawyers called solicitors?' Ben asks. 'Is bail called bail?'

Mom shoots Ben a look.

'I'll be fine,' I tell my mom, blinking my puffy eyes. 'You'll be proud of me.'

'I already am,' she says.

Grunting, Ben hauls my carry-on bag into the elevator.

'You sure you're only going to be gone a month?' he quips.

'Charles and Camilla may invite me fox hunting,' I say. 'I need to be ready for anything.'

Ben grins and runs one hand through his reddish hair. I smell the Chapstick on his lips. The fabric softener in his clothes. I feel . . . once again, I'm not sure *what* I feel. Is it love? The real deal? How can you know? And how can I allow myself to totally give my heart to a boy who's aiming for USC when I'm hoping for NYU? Can love survive forty-eight states of separation?

All I know for certain is, Ben is my favourite male name. Along with Brad (as in Pitt), Emile (as in Hirsch) and Johnny (as in, even-though-you're-old-enough-to-be-my-dad-you're-still-hot Depp). And, though Ben is my boyfriend, celebrities are still my first love. Plus, showing the world, along with *Scene*'s snooty editor-in-chief Nell Wickham, that a teen can get a great story, is still my life's goal. That and single-handedly reversing our country's double standard over weight. Why do girls have to look perfect to be popular, while boys can look so-so? My master plan is to expose the hypocrisy and give us curvy girls a break. Though that might take awhile.

True love? The *one*? Well, Mom says I'll know it when I feel it. Amelia agrees with her, even though she's only read about all-consuming passion in books. And, the one time I asked my dad when he knew he was truly in love with my mom, he said, 'When she was pregnant with you, I was constantly on the verge of tears.' Whatever *that* means. So, as far as I know, when I'm absolutely positively in love, I'll stop questioning it and start feeling it. At least that's what I'm hoping.

'Let's get this show on the road,' Dad says from inside the elevator.

Mom hugs and kisses me and brushes lint off my shirt. She tucks hair behind my ear, then hugs me again. When she finally lets me go, I fight the urge to rush past the open elevator door and run down the stairs so she can't cling to my leg. Now I see why Mel hates goodbyes. They last forever. Wouldn't it be nicer if goodbyes were a few seconds long and hellos went on for hours?

Finally, Ben and I are downstairs on the aromatic streets of Manhattan, climbing into my dad's car. My father is not only driving me to the airport, he's driving *Ben* and me. Unlike Amelia, Ben is *totally* into good-byes. He insisted on escorting me all the way to airport security. And, though we both have our driver's licences, neither one of us is old enough to drive in the city without an adult. So my dad offered to be our limo driver. In the family's Subaru.

'Everybody and every*thing* in?' Dad asks.

'Check,' I say.

'Away we go.'

Ben sits in the front passenger seat, while I sit in the back with my sunflowers and overstuffed handbag. My dad offered to play 'chauffeur' and let us both sit in the back seat, but how weird is that? Ben and I are going to make out with my father stealing glances in the rear-view mirror? I don't think so.

As we drive towards the Hudson River, I see the pier lights twinkling off the grey-blue water. Across the river, the sun has set behind the New Jersey skyline. I wonder what sunsets will look like in London. Will I miss the Hudson each time I see the Thames?

'Traffic looks good,' Dad says. 'We'll be there in no time.'

Riding down the West Side Highway, I flash on the last time I took this drive. There was snow on the ground, Keith Franklin, *Scene*'s hottie photographer was asleep next to me in the town car, and I was on my way to Hollywood. What a difference a year makes. I feel like I've lived a whole lifetime since then.

Ben says, 'There's usually a clog at the tunnel.'

Dad asks, 'Are they still doing construction?'

Ben answers, 'My mom says there's always construction on the Brooklyn Queens Expressway.'

'She's right,' Dad replies. 'Same with the Long Island Expressway.'

'What about the Grand Central Parkway?'

'Not as bad as the Van Wyck Expressway.'

I roll my eyes. What is it with guys and traffic? They love to talk about it. Not that I'm complaining. Actually, I'm happy to sit here quietly and let my mind drift into the land of Babble. I haven't admitted this to anyone, but I'm a tad nervous. Not freaking out yet, but definitely in the neighbourhood. I've spent so long trying to convince Nell I have what it takes, she totally stunned me by actually believing it. That old saying, 'Beware of what you ask for, you may get it' keeps rolling around in my head.

'Suck it up.'

'Suck what up?' Ben asks.

My eyes pop open. 'Did I say that out loud?'

He nods and laughs. Reading my mind, Dad says, 'By the time you get to London, Susanna, it'll be tomorrow and your nerves will be a thing of the past.'

I smile and inhale and hope he's right.

At the airport, we check my big suitcase in, and
Ben hoists my carry-on over his shoulder. I clutch my
flowers. Dad gets out of the car long enough to say
goodbye in typical Dad-style.

'Any liquids over three ounces in your carry-on?' he
asks me.

'No.'

'Scissors?'

'Nope.'

'Swords or spear guns?'

Clearly, my father downloaded and read the entire
list of prohibited items. Patiently, I say, 'No, Dad. And
I'm not bringing a machete on board, either.'

'Good. Then you're all set.'

In my father's hug, I feel how proud he is of me.
Sure, he'd rather I became a marine biologist the way
I'd planned after we visited Sea World together when
I was a kid. And, no, he wasn't thrilled that I could
name the cast members of *Grey's Anatomy* more easily
than the four longest bones in the body. Plus, he
definitely wasn't happy when I once fantasised out
loud about having Orlando Bloom's baby whether we

were married or not. But now, in his arms, I feel his respect for me. I had a dream, and I'm living it.

'Don't gawk too much when you're walking around London,' Dad says. 'You don't want to look like a tourist.'

'But I *am* a tourist,' I say.

He replies, 'Just don't look like one. Tourists are targets.'

With a kiss on my cheek, my father says goodbye and tells Ben to call him when he's ready. Then he heads for the parking lot. Which is proof that my dad is awesome. To give Ben and me a few moments on our own, he isn't going into the airport terminal with us. Instead, he'll park at a meter and wait for Ben to see me off on his own. Something I'm partly glad for and partly not. I wish I were in London already, not trying to figure out the perfect way to say goodbye to the boy who's my boyfriend but not absolutely, positively my one-and-only true love.

Together, Ben and I enter the air-cooled terminal. It smells faintly of sweat. I already have my boarding pass, so the only thing left to do is make our way to the security line.

'You have your passport?' Ben asks me, in a perfect imitation of my dad. 'Don't go flashing it around.'

I laugh. Ben chuckles, too, though I can tell he's nervous. Which makes me even more anxious. Suddenly, all I want to do is drop my sunflowers and run.

'This is it,' I say at the security checkpoint.

'Susanna—' Ben starts. But I stop him. I'm afraid I know what he's about to say. Three words I'm not ready to hear.

'I don't think they'll let me take these flowers on board,' I say quickly.

Ben takes the flowers back, and I lift my carry-on bag off his shoulder.

'Susanna,' he starts again.

'I love the flowers, Ben,' I say. 'And I love that you gave them to me.'

At that moment, Ben's eyes get very serious. My eyes go wide. I see what's coming. My heart surges with blood.

'I've gotta go,' I say, giving him a quick kiss on the lips. Then I turn and race-walk to the metal detectors. 'I hate goodbyes.'

'Wait!' Ben calls after me.

'I can't,' I shout, waving. I feel my cheeks flush and my shoulder sag under the weight of my bag. But, most of all, I feel grateful that there isn't any traffic in the security line so I can speed right through.

FOUR

I, Susanna Barringer, am pond scum. I'm an awful human being. The lowest of the low. Along with my heavy carry-on bag, even heavier guilt weighs me down as I pass fellow travellers on my way to the gate.

'What is your *problem*, Susanna?' I mutter under my breath.

Even *I* don't get it. I've wanted a boyfriend my whole life. Well, at least my whole teenage life. And boyfriends don't get any better than Ben. He's sweet, cute, supportive. He brings me sunflowers and walks me all the way to security! But, is he *it*? The big 'L'? We've never said those three words to each other: I love you. But Ben was about to. I could feel it. How could I hear those three words and not answer the same three words back?

Beware of what you wish for . . .? My heart sinks as I plod to the gate. Am I one of those girls who thinks

24

the grass is always greener? How could I be so shallow my first time on the lawn?

I sigh.

Maybe love is an unsure emotion. Perhaps my mom is wrong: You really *don't* know when you know.

Suddenly, as I pass a news-stand, my eye spots the cover photo on the latest *Scene* magazine.

'Britney is at it again,' I say to myself. Then I wonder, do they even care about Britney in Britain? What about Tomkat, Brangelina, and Gyllenspoon? Do they have their very own celebs? God, I hope it's not Victoria and David Beckham. Vicid? Davia? The Hams?

As deliberately as Victoria Beckham's lame attempt to take America by storm, I decide to pull a Scarlett O'Hara and think about Ben *tomorrow*. Or the next day. Or next month . . . after I've blown the lid off London.

Yes. That's what I'll do.

I wish I could remember every detail of the flight across the Atlantic: the on-board movie, the gooey pasta marinara they served for dinner, the way to manually inflate my life vest. But I sleep through most of it. Okay, I wake up long enough to eat the pasta, which is how I know it was a gelatinous mass of starch and cheese. And I do memorise the safety instructions on the card in front of my seat. But, as soon as the lights dim on board, the steady hum of the engines puts me right to sleep. I miss the movie entirely, waking up to the announcement that we are beginning our descent.

'Ironic, isn't it, the terms they use when you're thirty thousand feet in the air?' the man next to me says. 'Terminal. Descent. Hardly confidence-inspiring.'

He's about my dad's age, English, and pale to the point of translucence. I smile weakly at him, and tighten my seatbelt.

'Do you really think that flimsy strap will protect you?' he asks.

Again I flash on my trip to Hollywood. On that flight, I sat next to a poopy baby and her mother. I think I prefer that to the British Grim Reaper.

'This is my first trip to England,' I say brightly, changing the subject.

'Hopefully, it won't be your last,' he replies.

The plane banks left and passes through a feathery cloud layer. Below, I see tiny houses all squished together. In the distance, I spot patches of every imaginable shade of green.

I can't stop smiling.

The man beside me grunts. 'We're late,' he mumbles.

I ignore him. No one is going to ruin the day that I, Susanna Barringer, become an international reporter.

We land with a soft bounce and a long, strong brake. My seatmate doesn't exhale until we're slowly rolling for the gate. My heart is pounding. I'm here. On another continent. The empire from which our original thirteen colonies broke free. The motherland.

'When you cross streets in London,' the man beside me says, 'look the *opposite* way you would naturally look.'

The plane comes to a stop and everyone gets up at once.

'If you don't,' he says, 'you'll step directly into the path of a lorry.'

'What's a lorry?' I ask.

He rolls his eyes and says, 'Americans.' Then he exits the plane leaving me to chuckle over the fact that even in England – the land of Shakespeare, the Beatles and Simon Cowell – guys talk about traffic.

The first thing I do when I set foot on British soil is inhale deeply. Does London smell like New York? Though few cities are as pungent as my own, I take a big sniff inside the airport. Amazingly, Heathrow's aroma is nothing like JFK's. I smell floral perfume. All over. Not just wafting up from some old lady. The very air is scented. It's nice, like I'm walking through Victoria's Secret.

'Mind the pushchair,' a woman calls behind me.

I turn and see a mother and her baby stroller trying to get through the crowd. As I step to the side, she races onto a people mover ahead. Soon, she's swallowed up in the crowd. We're all moving in the same direction – down a narrow hallway, up an escalator, around a corner, down a ramp, on another people mover, down a bigger ramp. The straps on my Payless platform sandals dig into my puffy feet. My carry-on bag feels even heavier than it did in New York.

'Is this the way to baggage reclaim?' I ask a fellow passenger. After a while, it feels like I'll be *walking* all the way into central London.

'Yes,' she says.

Then I ask her one more question. 'What's a lorry?'

She laughs. 'I believe you call it a truck.'

'Got it.' I nod. 'Thanks.'

'Cheers.'

Though we both speak the same language, I quickly see that I have a lot more Britspeak to brush up on.

The signs over my head tell me I'm close to baggage reclaim. But, I still walk forever – past a duty free shop full of cigarettes and Jack Daniel's and, yes, perfume. I'm sorry to say that I can instantly spot the Americans. They (we?) are rounder than everybody else and taking photos of every dumb little thing with camera phones. When did we decide to experience reality only through a lens? I wonder. Will the memory centre of our brains shrivel up and die unless we have a photo to remind us where we were?

A security guard politely asks the camera-happy Americans to *stop* taking photos. It's not allowed in the airport. Embarrassingly, the Americans protest.

'Damn terrorists,' I hear one say. 'They've ruined everything.'

As I keep walking, I see an internet booth ahead. No way am I passing up this opportunity to email Amelia and Ben and my parents. Though I'm carrying mostly traveller's cheques, I cashed one in for British pounds before I left New York. So I use some of my British money to quickly send a message to all three: 'I'm here. You're there. More details soon. Cheers!'

Logging off, I rejoin the sea of passengers heading for baggage reclaim. After several more minutes, it feels like I'm walking the entire perimeter of the airport. I'm halfway around the world and it's beginning to feel like it. My chewing gum is beyond dead and I'm dying to spit it out. But there are no trash cans to be found anywhere. There's no trash, either. Is this a garbage-free country? Is everything recycled? Wouldn't *that* be nice?

At last, I retrieve my luggage and drag it through customs. Then I hear a sound that stuns me to my core.

'Susanna!'

It can't possibly be Nell's sister, I think, *she got my name right on the very first try.*

'Susanna Barringer!'

Wheeling around, I come face to face with Nell Wickham's younger sister, Blythe. She flings both arms around me and says, 'You're absolutely adorable!'

I pull back. This is Nell's *sister*?

Right away, though I'm ashamed to admit it, I notice that she's a little hefty. Not obese *à la* Disney World vacationers, but definitely womanly and padded. Her cheeks are two red pomegranates. Her hair is grey and falling to her shoulders in a mass of unkempt curls. She's clearly never had her teeth bleached, her nose fixed, her laugh lines Botoxed nor her toes squished into Manolo Blahniks from the fashion closet.

I love her instantly.

'The flight wasn't too dreadful, was it?' Blythe asks.

'Not at all,' I say. 'But I am dying to find a trash can for my gum.'

'You won't find a rubbish bin in the airport.'

For the second time that morning, I see how terrorism has affected another country. Is this a peek at our future? I wonder. Will New Yorkers *carry* their garbage around JFK?

Blythe holds her hand out. 'Give it to me,' she says. 'I'll hold it in my handbag until we get home.'

I just stare. Nell's sister wants me to spit my used gum into her hand? Have I landed on Mars?

'Suit yourself,' Blythe says, retracting her hand.

'Here, let me help with your bag,' Blythe says. 'I'm sure it's heavy.'

'How do you know that?'

'Unlike those anorexic twits that kiss Nell's arse, you are a girl of substance.'

Like I said, I love her *instantly*.

FIVE

It's a gorgeous, sunny summer day. Central London, the city part, is miles away from the airport. Or should I say kilometres? Not that I know how long a kilometre is. A mile plus a little? A mile minus a little? Really, I should have spent less time watching *America's Next Top Model* and more time studying the culture of my international destination.

'Shall we motor out of the car park and stop for petrol before joining the lorries on the dual carriageway?' I say.

At least I learned the lingo.

Blythe bursts out laughing.

'I've been studying your language so I wouldn't seem like an American,' I say.

Blythe laughs even harder. 'There's nothing *more* American than thinking you can change who you are by changing a few silly words.'

My shoulders sag.

'Though I do appreciate the effort,' she adds. 'And we do need petrol.'

Blythe pulls into the nearest gas station and I insist on paying. The exchange rate is about two for one. Meaning every two dollars is one pound.

'Gas prices aren't too bad here,' I say, reading the pump.

Blythe shoots me a look. 'You're joking, right?'

'One pound per gallon. That's only about two bucks, right?'

'It's one pound per *litre*.'

My mind sprints to the size of a litre of Coke and a gallon of milk. I gulp. A gallon is *much* bigger.

'And this banger has a huge tank,' says Blythe.

She doesn't need to tell me that a 'banger' is an old car. I have eyes. There are dents and dings on all four corners of her car. And she's not kidding about the gi-normous gas tank. The numbers on the petrol pump add up insanely fast. By the time the tank is full, my cash is gone.

'Americans always get a shock the first time they fill up,' Blythe says.

We hit the road at warp speed. Blythe drives from the *passenger* side of the front seat, on the *left* side of the road and as fast as a getaway car. She flies around circular roundabouts like a pinball. It's all I can do to keep from yelping each time she makes a turn and it looks like she's headed straight into oncoming traffic.

'Is there a speed limit here?' I ask, swallowing hard.

'Yes,' Blythe says. 'But I prefer using my horn.'

Blythe toots the hooter.

'Ah,' I say. Then I make a mental note for my *Teen Scene* magazine article: don't let our shared language fool you. Our two countries are worlds apart.

With Blythe at the wheel, and me on the edge of my seat, we zoom past a McDonald's restaurant that looks like an old Tudor-style house, a row of narrow homes that look like Brooklyn, and miles of wide green fields with grazing sheep that look like, well, England. Even though I'm rested, I feel travel grime all over me. After all, I did fly through the night, sleep in my clothes, and neglect to brush my teeth on the plane. My gum now tastes like Silly Putty and my hair hangs like limp spaghetti. I can't wait to get to Blythe's house so I can take a long, hot shower.

'Ashton, my village, is just ahead,' Blythe says.

'Ashton? Like Kutcher?'

'Who?'

I laugh. 'Are you *sure* you and Nell are really sisters?'

'Sometimes I wonder myself.'

Though I'm dying to visit London, I'm thrilled to see a real-life English village. And Ashton is a picture postcard. It's *gorgeous.* The old stone buildings are ginger-coloured, with peaked roofs, red flower boxes and lacy window curtains. The cobblestone streets look like flattened grey corn on the cobs. All smooth squarish stones laid *almost* in a row. I hear a church bell in the distance, smell burning hay. We pass a pharmacy, a post office, a library and a fish and chip shop, all housed in quaint structures that have been standing for centuries. Not a Duane Reade in sight. I feel like I've not only crossed the Atlantic, but I've travelled back in time, too. If they plucked out the cars and replaced them with horses and carriages, you could easily imagine bumping into Jane Austen.

'You live here?' I say, agog.

'No,' Blythe replies. 'I live *here.*'

She steers her car into a pebble-covered parking lot and cuts the engine. I look through the windshield and read the sign. The Red Fox Pub.

'You live in a *bar*?' I ask.

'Bit of a surprise?'

'Um, yeah.'

'Nell didn't want to tell your parents you'd be living in a room over a bar. Sounds a bit sordid if you look at it like an American. But you're not in the States now. So, come on, grab your luggage if you can lift it, and let me show you to your room.'

My tiny tiptoe into adulthood suddenly seems like a giant leap. I've never even *been* in a bar. How cool is this?

The Red Fox pub is an old two-storey brick building that looks like it was once a house. The pitched roof extends down to the first floor. Its tiles are old and patchy. Three pointy dormer windows pop out from the steep slope. All are surrounded by bright green ivy. On the ground floor, a huge picture window is open to the sunshine. On either side of the glossy black front door, two big round terracotta pots billow over with pink and purple flowers.

'Your room is upstairs,' Blythe says.

Rolling my suitcase over the gravel, I follow her through the front door. Downstairs is the bar. Or *pub*, I should say. Even though it's still morning, two men are drinking tall glasses of dark brown beer. A woman is sipping tea, while a couple of slices of toast cool in a stand that looks like a metal ribcage. Another woman, with a baby on her lap, is eating oatmeal. It's sunny and bright inside – not at all the way I imagine an American bar to look. The walls are panelled in a honey-tinted wood. And, even though a stuffed red fox is tucked into a corner, snarling with his sharp teeth bared, it feels friendly. (Though it does occur to me that red foxes may be endangered. Can you just stuff them and use them for decoration?)

'Your new American?' the bartender asks Blythe.

He's about my grandfather's age, with a shaggy grey moustache and seriously tanned skin. Even though it's warm out, he wears a brown suede vest over his long-sleeved denim shirt.

'Give us a hand, will you?' Blythe says to him.

He steps out from behind the bar and lifts my heavy bags as easily as I'd lift a gallon of milk. Or, I now know, nearly four litres of petrol.

'I'm Blythe's fella, Percival,' he says.

'Percival?'

'Named after one of King Arthur's Knights of the Round Table. But you can call me Percy. Everyone does.'

Percy climbs the steep, narrow staircase and I follow him. Blythe wisely chooses to stay downstairs. The hallway upstairs is even narrower than the curved stairwell. And, unlike the sun-flooded pub, the hall is dimly lit with one weak bulb. Percy walks to the far end and opens a door.

'Your room,' he says, tossing my bags inside my new home. 'The loo is down the hall, meals are in the pub. Settle in, then come downstairs for tea and toast. Any questions?'

'I heard that King Arthur's Round Table looked like a giant dartboard. Is that true?'

Percy laughs. I can see the gold fillings in his back teeth.

'It is,' he says. 'You and I are going to get on brilliantly.'

SIX

I'm here. I can't believe it! My room is a small alcove tucked beneath the corner of the roof. Even by New York City standards, it's tiny. I can barely fit myself and my suitcase on the floor. The only window looks out onto the car park. A quilted bedspread covers the single metal bed. A stack of stiff white towels sits on top of it. In the corner, a dark wood armoire is my closet. The only other furniture is a small bedside table with a lamp and a stack of books. No TV, no radio, no computer. The only sound I hear is the muted mutterings of the people downstairs in the bar.

I love it. It's so ... so ... British!

Hoisting my suitcase onto the bed, I leave it there to unpack later. Right now, I need to use the loo and finally find a rubbish bin for my chewing gum. A little make-up wouldn't hurt, either. And a comb. Though the moment I catch a glimpse of myself in the armoire mirror, I realise a minor touch-up won't even come close to repairing my appearance. A major overhaul is desperately needed. My hair is flat and stringy, my breath is gamey and my deodorant stopped working somewhere over the Atlantic. Tea and toast will have to wait. No way am I launching my career as an international reporter looking like this. Talk about an ugly American!

Unfortunately, the door to the loo is locked. I hear someone inside. Which bums me out since I was hoping finally to have a bathroom to myself. Oh well, I think, shrugging. Just like our New York apartment. Though I'm fairly certain I won't be sharing *this* bathtub with three toddlers and an entire family of rubber duckies.

'Susanna?' Blythe calls to me from the bottom of the stairs. 'I've made you breakfast.'

'Coming,' I say.

Then I dash into my room for my camera, pen and notebook so I can descend the stairs, not as a teen from the United States, but as a reporter who's ready to work. A grimy reporter who's seriously in need of a shower, but a reporter nonetheless. My British invasion has officially begun. From now on, I'm on assignment for *Teen Scene* magazine. Maybe Prince William has a secret royal cottage nearby? Perhaps David Beckham has brought his wife, Stick Spice, back to their home country? Does Kate Moss get inspiration for her new fashions from the vibrant green hills of England's countrysi—

'Susan?'

My heart stops. My stomach plummets. I recognise that voice.

'Good God, I thought *my* room was small.'

Standing in my open doorway, between me and my brilliant international career, is Francesca – the skinny, snotty, stuck-up assistant from *Scene* magazine. She peers at me over gazillion-dollar sunglasses from the fashion closet.

'What are *you* doing here?' I ask, amazed.

'Didn't Nell tell you?'

'Tell me what?'

My mouth is suddenly as dry as my flaky skin after the six-hour flight.

'Did you really think Nell Wickham would send you to London alone?' Francesca asks, sneering.

'You're my chaperone?'

'Hardly,' she says. 'I'm your boss. Your supervisor. Your superior. Every possible position *above* you. While you're here, you report to me.'

I feel the blood drain from my face.

41

'There must be some mistake,' I say. 'Nell specifically said she wanted my take on life in London. She never said anything about you.'

'Yes, well, I brought her to her senses. I mean, c'mon, you're a kid.'

'You're not much older than me,' I say, indignantly. 'Besides, I'm the Girl in the Trunk! I've walked the red carpet on Oscar night!'

Francesca scoffs. 'And now you're my loo mate.'

'Loo mate?' I swallow.

Groaning, she says, 'Yes. I'm staying in this dump with you. Which reminds me, the bathroom is mine from seven to eight each morning, and ten to eleven each night. Stay out of it.'

'But—'

'No exceptions. Though, frankly, Sue, you could use a shower and shampoo right now. And, *puh-leese*, spit out that gum. You're not in Queens anymore.'

Before I can tell her that I *don't* live in Queens and that my family lived in the meatpacking district of Manhattan long before it was cool, Francesca – the emaciated witch who's the true Mini-Me of Nell – tosses me a rail pass and says, 'Meet me at the village train station in an hour. Don't make me wait.'

'Blythe made breakfast,' I splutter.

Francesca dramatically rolls her eyes. 'Believe me, Susan, missing a meal won't kill you.'

Flushed, I say, 'My name is *Susanna*. With two Ns and two As.'

'What*ev*.'

Off she goes in a swirl of pale pink fluff with her Jimmy Choo shoes and her Louis Licari highlights and her Furla ivory leather 'Greta' tote.

Looking every bit as fresh and pretty as I wish I did.

Why, oh, why did I bring so many black shirts and black pants?

SEVEN

Maybe it's jet lag, or the weak coffee and cold white toast I gulped down in the pub, or the fact that I'm sitting here, in the tiny village train station, completely grubby, totally on time though Francesca is totally late, but a tsunami of homesickness passes over me. I miss my brothers' flyaway hair, and the smell of Ben's Chapstick. I miss Amelia's daily rant on the ridiculous cost of college. I even miss Nell. A little. At least I never had to sit with Nell Wickham on a train into the city. Which is what I'm about to do with Francesca. If she ever shows up.

'American?' one of my fellow waiting-room travellers asks. We're both sitting on a bench in the glass-enclosed stop.

'Is it that obvious?' I say.

'Your shoes,' she answers.

I look down at my Reebok sneakers and sigh.

'My best friend warned me,' I say. 'But I'm hoping

to find some cool new shoes in the city.'

'Topshop,' she says.

At first, I think she's giving me some British greeting like 'top of the morning!' or 'Cheerio!' It flashes through my mind that she's waiting for an Americanesque response like, 'Yo, dude, wuzzup?'

Then I remember.

'Topshop!' I squeal. 'Yes!'

The British store took New York City by storm a few months ago, but I've never been in it. Supposedly, it's the 'must-shop' store for teens, which is why I've passed it up. After my experiences at Fashion Week, the only 'must' I have for fashion is that I *must* think for myself. No way am I letting a fashion designer get rich on my attempts to look like everybody else.

Still, it would be cool to see the original store. Definitely a 'must-go' for a teen reporter.

'Oxford Circus,' the woman on the bench says. 'You can't miss it.'

At that moment, Francesca pulls her rental car into Ashton station. Lurching across the pebbled parking lot in her Choos, she joins me in the waiting area, breathless.

'Damn country roads! My car got stuck in the mud.'

'Car?' I say. 'The station is only a three-block walk from the pub.'

Francesca glares. 'I don't *do* walking.'

Sneering at my huge white Reeboks, she adds, 'If I had to wear those hideous shoes, I'd cut off my feet.'

'What*ev*,' I say, leaping up as soon as the train pulls into the station. Turning to the English woman in the waiting room, I thank her for the great tip. Then I bound onto the train the minute the doors swoosh open.

Take *that*, Mr Choo.

British trains, I discover, are just like New York City subways. Except that the seats are cushioned, there's no graffiti etched into the windows, and they don't smell like dirty socks. And, of course, they're above-ground, chugging through the most beautiful scenery ever.

'Damn.'

Oh, yeah, and they're crowded. Francesca sits in the only other available seat – directly across from me. Ugh. Not only do I have to look at her, I have to listen to her cursing her BlackBerry. Like swearing at it will magically produce a signal.

'Crap,' she says, even louder.

Annoyed, I want to remind her that we're guests in this country, representing the United States. But that would let the other passengers know that we're together. So I tuck my huge boat feet under the seat and stare out of the window.

England flashes by my eyes in a slide show of green. I've never seen more vibrant shades of grass. The sheep look like giant cotton-wool balls with feet. The sky is a vast canopy of non-stop blue. My heart is pounding. Once again, I can't believe I'm actually here. In England. *Me*. Susanna Barringer!

'Shit.'

Francesca slams her BlackBerry again, but I ignore her and smile. Who cares about a silly signal when I know exactly where I'm going to get my first international scoop?

EIGHT

Oxford Circus is exactly that – a circus. It's a big round intersection on Oxford Street, surrounded by pretty old buildings. The sidewalks are packed with people and their shopping bags. The street is wide. Times Square without the neon. Classier than Canal Street, less snobby than Madison Avenue. I see a string of familiar stores: H&M, Benetton, Sketchers, the Body Shop, Starbucks.

Don't ask me how I got here. Somehow, I did. I passed shiny black doors with gleaming brass knobs, long yellow flower beds, red phone booths. I waited at traffic lights with little white arrows. I explored British-sounding streets like Earlham and Royalty Mews. I walked through London's Soho district, which is like New York's Chelsea or the East Village with guys holding hands and shops selling black leather. And, of course, I had to stop in a tiny park and eat my pasty. Which was warm and oniony and reminded me of a New York City knish. Both taste delicious but end up sitting in your stomach like a potato rock.

But, I made it. I'm here. On Oxford Street. In the middle of the circus. Practising my training as a native New Yorker: the ability to 'stare' at people without actually looking them in the eye. In other words, I have the innate talent to completely size someone up with one quick glance. Sure, some might call it being 'judgemental', but who's being judgemental then? Besides, a little judgement goes a long way in a city. How many gazelles would there be in the wild if they couldn't use their judgement to sprint at the first whiff of a cheetah?

People stride past me, red double-decker buses belch out exhaust. I walk down the street with my head held high, my shoulders on a hanger, and both eyes open for celebrities and the latest teen scene. It's awesome. I feel free. Invigorated. Unencumbered by Francesca's sneer. I'll show her. I'll show them all. I, Susanna Barringer, don't need a boss, supervisor *or* a superior. I'm the Girl in the Trunk! I get the story no matter *what*.

Fab!

The cell signal must be fine here in London. Just like

New York, nearly everyone has a phone pressed up to one ear. As I walk, I catch snippets of conversation.

'. . . be there by half past.'

'. . . on holiday until next week . . .'

'. . . so yeah, bring your mates.'

My mom was right. The British accent makes everyone sound so nice!

I walk down a side street, circle back up another, then continue covertly checking everyone out. Like the girl with the nose ring, there's a vague punkiness to many of the kids my age – their jeans are super-skinny, their hair is spiked with gel, their eyeliner is black. Nobody looks overly smiley. There are a lot of Indian women in brightly-coloured saris, and almost everyone has a better haircut than I do. Mostly, though, I learn a lot about the English in Oxford Circus by looking at their *shoes*. Flats, sandals and sneakers. Not quite as boaty as my Reeboks, or as high as my Payless platforms, but definitely comfy walking shoes. Nobody spends their rent on their feet. Francesca would look ridiculous in her gazillion-dollar Jimmy Choos.

Suddenly, I'm glad I'm wearing basic black, on my curvy body. I even embrace my dirty hair and the chin zit that resurfaces, in the same spot, every month like clockwork. I'm *real*. A human being. I'm no Barbie doll.

Right there, in the middle of Oxford Circus, I firm up my resolve to refine my *inner* beauty. Who wants to look like a mannequin? Slavishly following every fashion trend. Not me. Not the Girl in the Trunk. I, Susanna Barringer, have my own style. It's called *substance*. From this moment on, I say to myself, I'm going to cultivate the look of someone who'd rather spend her money saving the polar bears in the North Pole than decorating her South Beach dieted body with insanely expensive fashion trends that will be *so* over next seas—

'Hey! Topshop!'

Ahead, rising up like Emerald City, is the store I've come to see . . . I mean, *report* on. Floods of teens are pushing through the glass front doors. Even more are spitting out of the exit onto Oxford Street with billowing shopping bags, wearing fashion trends that will be so over next season.

My stomach drops. They look amazing! Why, oh why, did I wear humungous white Reeboks?

With my heart beating into my basic black shirt and my cheeks flushed, I inhale deeply. On the exhale, I set my jaw and state, 'I'm going in.'

International career – here I come. Pulling my notepad and a pen out of my handbag, I look right (because I *feel* like looking left) and cross the busy street into my destiny.

NINE

Topshop is *awesome*. In the true sense of the word. Not as in, 'Fergie has an awesome singing voice', but genuine jaw-dropping awe. Which is exactly what my jaw does. *Drop*. The moment I pass through the glass front doors of the store, a tidal wave of sounds, sights and smells slams into me, making it impossible to close my gaping mouth.

'This two-for-one rack is brilliant!' I hear someone say through the pounding beat of the loud music.

Two for one! Suddenly, my quest for inner beauty takes a back seat to my outer desire to look hot. Or, if not actually *hot*, then cooler than the dark trousers, shirt and humungous white Reeboks I'm wearing.

Shoes! Yes, that's what I need. New shoes to disguise my Americanism and help me blend in. Should I buy skinny jeans too, I wonder? For professionalism's sake?

Like being sucked into a giant black hole, the

gravitational pull of the Kate Moss section is too strong to resist. Sorry, polar bears.

'Excuse me,' I say. 'Pardon me. Oops . . . was that your foot?'

Girls and their moms wiggle through the clothing racks like worms in a bait can. Large flat-screen televisions against the walls broadcast a non-stop catwalk show. It smells of cherry lipgloss and the faint scent of oestrogen – the aroma of females stalking a bargain. I stash my pen and notebook in my handbag and leap right in.

Instantly, I get why everyone loves this store. The styles are hot, the atmosphere is cool and everything seems to be on sale. Briefly, I'm ashamed at how quickly I abandon my anti-fashion statement. But, just as quickly, I justify it by telling myself it's my *job* to immerse myself in the British teen scene. And Topshop is clearly its epicentre.

Sweet!

'Kate would wear punky chain sandals with that net dress,' I overhear a girl tell her friend.

'Brilliant! Grab me a pair of size fives, will you?'

Size five shoes? I try not to feel like a lumbering cow as I weave through the crowd towards the shoe section. Not that I ever get there. On the way to de-Americanising my feet, I spot the chance to Britishify my body – on sale! There's an entire rack of discounted Kate Moss styles that are ideal for launching my international career.

Awesome!

As I pull three size ten skirts and one pair of jeans called 'Ziggy' off the rack, I wonder if wearing Kate Moss designs means you have to date rock stars. Too bad Paolo Nutini is taken. Or is he?

Chuckling as I head for the dressing room, I flash on Ben. He's about as far from a rock star as you can get. Ben is more Steven Spielberg than Justin Timberlake. Of course, *I'm* more Steven Spielberg than Kate Moss. Still, is that what's missing? The rock star factor? Is that why I'm having such a hard time taking the leap into love? Ben is a nice, normal guy. Do I, Susanna Barringer, celebrity reporter *extraordinaire*, need more star quality?

'Get a grip, Susanna,' I mutter under my breath.

Just because I've ridden in a limo with Hollywood hottie Randall Sanders and (*pant, pant*) star photographer Keith Franklin, doesn't mean I'd ever actually have a hunk for a boyfriend. Not that Ben isn't cute. He is. It's just that he's no rock star. Is that why I'm holding on to my heart?

I groan. My inner dialogue can continue in this same loop all day. And I have serious work to do. Namely, British clothes to buy.

I'll think about Ben tomorrow, or next week. After I snag my first international scoop.

Inside my dressing-room cubicle, I untie my Reeboks and slip out of my slimming black pants. Before I can launch a mental attack on my *flabalicious* thighs, I slip into a Kate Moss skirt. *Try* to, that is. To my horror, it barely makes it past my knees. In fact, none of the size ten skirts I brought into the dressing room come even *close* to fitting me. And Ziggy? Well, I might as well try to wear something from Kate Moss's own closet. The jeans are tiny. And, in the glaring white light, I can't help but notice my butt is *so* not.

How did this happen? One pasty and I'm now an extra large? Mortified, I throw my own clothes back on, hang up Kate's miniature garments, and dash out of the dressing room. It's true! I scream inside my head. Americans *are* all obese! We just don't know it until we travel!

The pounding beat inside Topshop now feels like a hammer hitting my chest. I can't get out of there fast enough.

'Coming through,' I shriek as I push my way

through the crowded store for the sunlight outside. I don't stop until I'm back on Oxford Street, in the Circus, feeling as huge and American as my Reeboks.

TEN

I'm wiped out. I feel as though I just lived the longest day of my life. And it's not even over yet. At least the train ride back to Ashton is much quieter than it was this morning. Francesca isn't sitting across from me cursing her BlackBerry.

I'm heading back to my room over the pub for two things I desperately need: a long, hot shower and a nap. I can barely keep my eyes open. Amazingly, it's a struggle to stop my stomach from rumbling, too. That pasty seems like a distant memory. I'm hungry, tired, and longing for my four-inch platform shoes to make me feel taller and leaner. The dressing-room horror is still fresh in my mind. It's only Day One and I'm already down on myself.

I sigh.

How could I go from wanting to save the polar bears to feeling like a blubbery beached whale so quickly? In one store? What happened to the girl of substance?

My eyelids drooping, I decide to answer that question later. After I figure out what to do about Ben and how to write an awesome article for *Teen Scene* magazine. For now, I lean my head against the window and wait for the *chuga-chug, chuga-chug* of the train to drown out all thoughts of bears and beaches and jeans named Ziggy.

'Ashton. Next stop, Ashton.'

The announcement over the tannoy wakes me. Still groggy, I smooth my greasy hair and gather my stuff. I'm tempted to dig through my handbag for lipgloss and a comb, but why bother? I'll be in the shower in a few minutes anyway.

The train screeches slowly to a stop at Ashton station. It's still sunny out – a perfect summer's day. The faint scent of roses is in the air. I stretch and yawn and doubt I'll even make it into the shower before my nap. Walking through town on my way to the Red Fox pub, I pass two women on horseback. They wave; I wave back. A tiny car toots its horn at a golden retriever in its driveway. Birds tweet all around me. The sun feels like a warm kiss on my two cheeks. At that moment, the buzz of London feels as far away as Nell Wickham's white couch.

That's when I smell it.

'Fish and chips!' I squeal.

Ahead, I see a small, stone fish and chip shop with a red awning. The aroma of fried food is too enticing to resist. Instantly, I forget about the Ziggy nightmare. I'm working, after all. What better way to experience life as an English teen than to eat like one? Who needs to look like a model anyway? Why spend your life hungry?

Invigorated, I follow my nose through the shop door and stop dead.

'Zabar's?' I blurt out.

The man behind the counter is wearing a baseball cap with the name of a New York City gourmet store embroidered on it.

'You know it?' he asks me.

'I live in New York. Everybody in the city knows Zabar's,' I reply. 'Where did you get that hat?'

He laughs. 'At Zabar's, of course.' Then he turns to the kitchen in the back of the shop and yells, 'Ricky!'

A boy appears from the rear of the chip shop, wiping his hands on a long, white apron tied around his waist. He wears a red T-shirt and blue jeans and has spiky bleached blond hair. He's older than I am. In his early twenties. The moment our gazes connect, every drop of blood drains from my face.

'Yeah?' Ricky says to his dad.

'We have a real New Yorker in our midst.'

Ricky chuckles and I feel dizzy. His smile curls up on one side of his face, while his intense green eyes bore two holes in my pupils. My head is spinning. I long to run my hand over the top of his head. Are those spikes sticky or soft? Are those real diamond studs in both earlobes?

'Ricky?' I splutter, standing there with my dirty, flat hair, pale lips and *gi-normous* Reeboks that make me look like an obese American.

'You were expecting a Nigel or a Cyril?' his dad says.

I laugh. A tad too hard.

Ricky is a hunk *and* a hottie. With an English accent, too. I wonder if he's in a rock band? Does he know James Blunt? Does he have a hidden tattoo? My skin starts to tickle.

At that moment, I want to reverse time and walk backwards to the train station. From there, I would walk straight home to the pub – past the chip shop – so I could nap, shower and blow-dry my hair before applying lipgloss and mascara and my slimming Payless platform shoes. Then, and only then, I'd saunter over to the little store with the red awning so I could oh-so-casually bump into the cutest boy in Ashton . . . maybe even England.

'My son Richard spent the first year of his sixth form on exchange in New York,' he says.

I nod. What's a sixth form? Not that it matters since I'm suddenly unable to stop nodding and grinning like a village idiot.

'I popped by Zabar's when I was in the States visiting him,' Ricky's dad continues. 'Nothing like that here, I'm afraid.'

He chortles. Ricky continues to stare into my eyes. Dare I say it, my *soul*. Still unable to form a complete sentence, I nod and grin. Ricky was on my home turf and I didn't even know it? I could have shown him the Statue of Liberty, the Empire State Building, my by-line in *Scene* magazine! I could have taken him to the Virgin Megastore in Times Square and hinted that I wasn't planning on remaining a virgin forever.

'What would you like, love?' Ricky's dad asks me.

My cheeks blush purple. Would I like love? Of course I'd like love. Deep, passionate, blinding, soul-melding love. The kind of love that makes you *sure*. Your pulse races, but your heart beats with the knowledge that he's the one.

'Fish and chips, then?' Ricky's dad asks me.

'Oh, yes,' I stammer, adding, 'A small.'

A giggle escapes my throat like a burp and I want to dip myself in fish batter and dive into the deep fryer. Mentally, I slap myself in the face.

Do you have to go brain-dead every time you meet a cute boy?!

Especially a boy whose awesome form – sixth or otherwise – was once in Zabar's.

Still red-faced, I stand there and try to stare without looking like I'm actually, well, *staring*. As Ricky returns to the kitchen to prepare my order, I reach up and fluff my hair, but I know it's a lost cause. Too late for lipgloss, too, so I bite both lips for colour and pray that Ricky is near-sighted.

'You must be one of the American girls staying at Percy's pub,' Ricky's dad says. Then he reaches his right hand over the counter and introduces himself. 'I'm Graham.'

'Susanna,' I say.

Graham shakes my hand and says, 'Welcome to our little corner of the world. We're all neighbours here. If there's anything you need or want, just let me know.'

How 'bout your son?

The question instantly pops into my head. Thank

goodness it stays there, instead of shooting out my mouth. I press my lips together to make sure nothing stupid has a chance to escape.

In a few minutes, Ricky emerges from the kitchen with my fish and chips. He gives me a look and a tiny flick of his head and my knees go soft. Who needs a rock star when a boy like Ricky is the boy (almost) next door?

ELEVEN

I, Susanna Barringer, am a wad of gum stuck to the bottom of life's shoe. I'm the lowest of the low. Not even two days away from Ben and I'm already panting over Ricky. Is it his accent, the way one eyebrow cocks when he looks at me, that lopsided smirk? Is it because he's an older boy who looks at me at all? What*ev*. All I know is I could walk under a snake with a top hat on – I've sunk that far.

Still . . .

Somehow I make it back to the Red Fox pub, carrying my fish and chips in a grease-spotted brown paper bag. I'm in a daze, shifting between bad-mouthing myself for my slutty lack of loyalty and imagining how Ricky's lips might taste. Like fries? Codfish? A field of wild sunflowers?

'Get a grip, Susanna,' I say again.

But, by the time I reach the pub, my whole life feels like it's slipping between my fingers.

'You made it home for tea!' Blythe greets me as I walk through the door.

I hold up my fish and chips and ask, 'Can I eat this in here?'

'Of course. Sit down. Want a Coke?'

I sigh. '*Diet* Coke, if you have it. Somehow, I've ballooned up overnight. I can't even squeeze into a size ten!'

'Size ten is tiny.'

'Yeah, right,' I say.

Blythe bursts out laughing 'You know that English sizes are different from American sizes, right?'

Instantly, I perk up. 'They are?'

'A British size ten is about an American size six.'

'It is?'

'Shoes, too. A British size seven is about an American eight and a half.'

Flinging my arms around Blythe, I squeal, 'You mean, I'm not an obese American with Bozo feet?'

She laughs again. 'Sit down in the bar and eat your food.'

Blythe goes to get me a soda while I choose a table by the window. My greasy fish and chips are still warm, the sun feels as hot as Ricky, and I can't wait to sink my teeth into my very first bite of authentic English foo—

'Where the hell have you been?'

The hairs on my neck stand up. I don't need to turn around to know who's standing behind me.

'I've been at work, Francesca. Where the hell have *you* been?'

Francesca slams a cell phone down on the table. Then she circles around my chair to face me. I can't help but notice she still looks fresh and fabulous. How does she do that? Does she check into a hotel for an afternoon shower and blow-dry? Slyly, I bite my lips again to give them a little colour. Then I focus on the imprint her sunglasses have made on the bridge of her nose and think, *that's the only part of you I like.*

'From now on,' Francesca says, 'carry this cell at all times.'

'A phone?' My eyes light up.

'Calm down, Miss Tween. It's a local phone only. You can't call your little BFFs in the States.'

Making a face, I'm tempted to inform her that I'm as far from being a tween as she is to ever getting married. But it sounds stupid and, yes, *tweeny*, even to me. Not everyone thinks marriage is so hot. In fact, by the time I'm ready to tie the knot, being hooked up with one guy forever will probably be *so* yesterday.

'What's that god-awful smell?' Francesca glares at my deep-fried meal.

'Research,' I say. Then I peel back the oily newsprint and take a huge bite of fish, celebrating the fact that in England, size tens are tiny.

It's hard to say what feels better. The hot water flowing over my body, or the anticipation of falling into a dead sleep in my single bed under the eaves. My whole being is so exhausted I can barely reach my arms overhead to wash my hair. Must be jet lag, I think. I haven't felt this wiped out since the same fatigue drained my energy in Hollywood. Thankfully, Francesca has left the building and Ricky's yummy fish and chips have quieted the grumbling beast inside my stomach. I can sleep straight through dinner. Or do they call it 'supper' here?

'Susanna?'

There's a knock on the bathroom door.

'Yes?' I say, poking my head around the shower curtain.

'You have a telephone call.'

I recognise Blythe's voice through the closed door.

'Could you please tell Francesca to give me a break?'

I say. 'I'm allowed to take a shower. It's in the company handbook.'

'It's not Francesca.'

Oh no, I think. It's Nell. Who else would call? My parents agreed to give me a few days to settle in before they hounded me for info. Neither Mel nor Ben have this number since we all decided IMs and emails were the best way to deal with the time difference. Did Francesca tell Nell I went to Oxford Circus on my own? That I refused to let her boss me around? Is she ratting me out already? That skinny bit—

'It's Ricky from the chip shop,' Blythe says. 'Shall I have him ring you later?'

'No!' I shriek.

Still soapy, I shut off the water and grab a towel. Wrapping it around my dripping body, I open the door.

'I'll talk to him,' I say, casually, blinking as the shampoo stings my eyes.

Blythe shakes her head and hands me the phone.

'Ricky?'

'Wuddup,' he says.

I nearly burst out laughing. The combination of street slang and an English accent is hilarious. Like a butler who moonlights as a gangster.

'Wuddup wit u?' I reply.

He chuckles. I can still picture his sideways grin. My towel nearly slips to the floor.

'You up for a pint?' he asks.

'A pint?'

'At the pub. *Wit* me.'

Now I chuckle. Nervously.

'I . . . uh . . .'

'You don't have to be twenty-one, if that's what you're worried about.'

It is.

'I'm not worried about anything,' I lie.

'The drinking age here is eighteen,' Ricky adds. 'And if you *look* eighteen, nobody asks for proof.'

I say, 'Oh. Well, then.'

Standing naked and soapy in my towel, I'm not sure how to respond. A few possibilities flash through my brain.

Of course I look eighteen!

I was eighteen years *ago.*

Is that eighteen in English years or American?

Instead, worried that Blythe will blow my cover, I ask, 'Is there another pub in town? Other than the Red Fox?'

Ricky laughs. 'We're going to a *real* pub. Meet me in

front of the chip shop in an hour and I'll show you where me and my mates hang out.'

'Excellent,' I say. Then I wince. *Excellent?* Am I a Mother Superior?

Ricky hangs up and I stand there, staring at my sudsy reflection in the bathroom mirror, praying I packed something that not only makes me look older, but hotter and not half-dead with exhaustion.

TWELVE

I wear black pants, a black shirt and my four-inch Payless platform shoes. What else do I have? I curse Sasha at *Scene* magazine for convincing me to stick to basic black. I look like a crow. Nothing like Kate Moss. But, as I apply the final swipe of cherry-red gloss to my lips and fluff my blown-dry hair, I'm excited to see that I look very nearly eighteen. The fatigue bags under my eyes add two years instantly.

Sweet!

'Where are *you* going?'

Francesca returns just as I'm walking out the front door.

'None of your beeswax,' I say, then immediately regret it.

'Beeswax?' She tosses her head back and scoffs. 'How quaint. Are you headed to the drive-in for a malted shake?'

'Don't you have some cave to hang upside-down in?' I say.

Francesca flips her hair in my face. My platforms wobble a bit on the pebbled driveway in front of the Red Fox pub, but I hold my head up and march towards the centre of Ashton. To meet my new mates. So there.

Ricky is standing exactly where he said he would. In front of his family's chip shop. It's just starting to get dark, which is good. Screaming white sunlight isn't flattering on anybody . . . not even Kate Moss.

'I made it,' I say, inexplicably out of breath. Like I travelled two miles, instead of two blocks, to get there.

'You look different,' Ricky says.

'I showered. And washed my hair. In fact, I was *in* the shower when you called.'

I wince again. *Good one, Susanna!* I screech inside my head. *He's now picturing you naked and covered in soap.*

'I mean, I was rinsed,' I say. 'I was just about to get out of the shower.'

Shut up! Shut up! Shut up!

I bite the inside of my cheeks to prevent my mouth from opening again. Ricky just stands there looking insanely cute. Out of his apron, I see that he's skinny. He changed his clothes, and is now wearing long shorts that extend to the middle of his calf. A tiny band of underwear elastic is visible. Not a big hip-hop puff. Just

73

enough to catch my eye each time I look him up and down. Striped ankle socks poke out of his black sneakers and a frayed braided bracelet encircles his wrist. His yellow T-shirt shows his ribcage. How can you be thin, I wonder, when you spend your days surrounded by fries?

'Can you walk in those?' Ricky asks, pointing to my platform shoes.

'Of course. See?'

Off I go, like a total tool, walking towards the centre of town. Frankly, it's harder than I thought. The cobblestones are treacherous. Plus, I suddenly discover that I've forgotten how to walk naturally when the hottest boy in Ashton is looking at my butt. Probably picturing it naked and sudsy, too.

'You coming?' I ask, turning around.

'The pub is this way,' he says, aiming his thumb in the opposite direction.

Oh.

I clomp back over the *wobble*stones and briefly wish I was taking that nap after all.

The *real* pub, where Ricky and his mates hang out, is called McQueens. Being a New Yorker, I would have assumed it was a gay bar. Or a hang-out in London's

Soho. But, as Ricky and I walk through the front door, I instantly see it's not. The moment my eyes adjust to the dim interior, I see a row of burly men hunched over huge glasses of dark brown beer. Two older girls are perched on their boyfriends' laps. A loud soccer game blares out from the television above the bartender's head.

I swallow hard. Clearly, I'm way out of my league. The girls snap their gum and eye me suspiciously. One is wearing a floral halterneck top without a much-needed bra; the other sports a skin-tight T-shirt with the image of a skull and crossbones and the words 'Urban Pirate' on it.

I wiggle my fingers in their direction, but neither girl waves back.

God, I hope these aren't Ricky's mates.

'Come meet my mates,' he says, walking straight for the table where the Urban Pirate is sitting. My stomach plummets.

'Two pints of Guinness,' Ricky says to the bartender over his shoulder. Then, as all the spit in my mouth instantly dries up, I follow Ricky to the table to meet his mates.

'This is Susanna,' he says, taking a seat. 'She's from America.'

The group grunts. I'm tempted to add that I'm a *New York* American – the ice-cream sundae of cities, with a cherry on top – not to mention a reporter for *Teen Scene* magazine and the infamous Girl in the Trunk. But no one seems to care. The guys keep watching the TV. The girls smile fakely and resume nuzzling their boyfriends' necks.

I sit. The bartender lines the beers up and Ricky pays for them. It's my first beer, ever, and it looks like a *root* beer. The thick foam at the top is caramel-coloured. I can't believe the bartender didn't card me. Ricky and his mates are obviously over eighteen. What's one more mate? Or maybe, my experiences in Hollywood and Fashion Week have matured me beyond my years. Perhaps Nell's abuse hardened my soft adolescent edges. I can't wait to tell Amelia! Not even in England a week and I already have a date with an older boy and a beer!

'Cheers,' I say, taking a hearty, celebratory gulp.

It's *awful*. Like drinking rotten apple juice. My throat closes and I'm afraid my stomach will send the beer right back up.

This is why American kids can't wait to reach twenty-one?

'Cheers,' Ricky replies, drinking nearly half his pint in three huge swallows. I can't look without wanting to retch.

'Ashton is awesome,' I say to the group, attempting to launch a conversation.

'It sucks,' one of the guys says.

The girls chime in. 'There's nothing to do here.'

'As soon as I save up, I'm moving to London.'

I nod, thinking, *it must be like living in New Jersey at home. So close to the centre of the world, yet an entire universe away.*

'Who's winning the soccer game?' I ask, brightly, looking up at the television set over the bar.

'It's called *football*,' one of the boys grumbles at me.

Both girls roll their eyes.

'Oops,' I say. 'I knew that.'

Then I quip, 'Though I hear David Beckham now calls it soccer.'

In a flash, the entire pub goes silent. I swear I can hear the faucet dripping behind the bar. One of the husky-backed men at the bar turns around and snorts at me. The boys at my table glare and the girls look like they want to scratch my eyes out.

Ricky mutters, 'We're still a little testy about losing him.'

'Ah,' I say. Then, desperate to save face, I add, 'Look on the bright side, you lost Posh Spice, too!'

THIRTEEN

There are few things in life I know for certain: I'll never be a model – super or otherwise – Orlando Bloom will never be my prom date, Nell will never permanently get my name straight, and Amelia will always be my BFF. And, one more thing: my date with Ricky was an utter disaster.

'Nobody calls her Posh Spice any more,' one of the girls said, rolling her eyes.

'You must be from *Kansas*, USA,' the other said.

Both tittered. Miss Urban Pirate asked me, 'What's with those clothes? Are you going to a funeral?'

'Or a costume party dressed as a black hole?'

Ricky's mates laughed behind their hands. Stupidly, I took another gulp of beer. It tasted even worse than my first mouthful.

'First pint?' one of guys asked, cackling.

'No,' I lied. 'I usually drink lager.'

The entire table erupted in laughter.

'Lager tastes like piss,' someone said.

'Recycled piss,' said another.

Ricky replied, 'Lay off.' But his friends just piled it on.

'She probably watches *American Idol*.'

'She probably wants to be *on American Idol*.'

'I'd rather listen to the dentist drilling my teeth,' one of the boys said in a spot-on imitation of Simon Cowell.

'Is there a category for best imitation of a black pudding?'

'Did you see those shoes? She looks like Frankenstein.'

Before I even realised I was doing it, I was on my Frankenstein feet, lurching out the door.

'Susanna!'

Outside, in the grey-blue light of the disappearing day, Ricky catches up with me.

'My friends are idiots,' he says.

'They're your *friends*?' I ask, agog. At that moment, I notice I'm dangerously close to tears. My cheeks are flushed and I can feel the sting around my eyes.

'They're just showing off,' he says. 'The jerks.'

Biting the inside of my lip, I will myself not to cry. Ricky puts one hand on my shoulder and I shake it off.

'I have to go to London early tomorrow,' I say. 'I need to get home.'

'Let me make it up to you.'

'No.'

'Please?'

'*No*.'

With that, I put my Payless platforms in high gear and race-walk back to the Red Fox pub. Never once looking back to see if Ricky is still watching.

FOURTEEN

Work takes my mind off Ricky and his icky mates. I spend several days with a map in my hand – walking around London, sweating, soaking everything up, searching for a scoop. While Francesca does *whatever* in the climate-controlled *Teen Scene* office, I'm on the streets. With my peeps. A reporter on a mission.

'What's your impression of American teens?'

'What do you think we think of you?'

'Have you ever been to the United States?'

Each day, I ask the same questions. Amazingly, I hear the same answers, too.

'You're all stuck-up. Conceited.'

'You think we're posh. Prim and proper.'

'Never been to the States, but I watch American television.'

So, I keep walking. Keep asking.

Like New York, London is a city of neighbour-hoods. Each with its own personality. I discover that

Hampstead is very highbrow, artsy Chelsea is more like New York's SoHo, though our Chelsea is like *London's* Soho, Kensington is where all the museums are, and Knightsbridge is where I'd like to live because it's in the centre of *everything*. As for celeb-spotting, well, it's a tricky business. Similar to New York, London celebs blend in. They walk among us. It's hard to know who you're seeing . . . unless, of course, you're professionally-trained like *moi*.

Today, I'm exploring Notting Hill. Yeah, I know Hugh Grant and Julia Roberts don't *really* live there, but Percy told me that a lot of real-live celebrities actually do.

'It's the Tribeca of London,' he said. 'I saw it on the telly.'

Thank God I'm wearing my Reeboks. I have yet to explore the subway . . . I mean, the *Tube*. How can you see anything underground? Besides, all this exercise is great for working off the pub food I've been snarfing down. I've scaled back on the pasties and the fish and chips, but Blythe makes a wild mushroom and lamb ragout that's totally kickin'.

It's just before noon. On my way to Notting Hill, I scan the streets for the London teen scene as well as the celebrity 'uniform': baseball cap, Chanel sunglasses, humungous handbag. I look for that certain something – a way of walking that looks like you're *trying* to be invisible. When you're not a celebrity, you don't have to make an effort to be ignored. You just are.

The temperature is warm, but it's raining. *Misting*, really. I feel silly holding an umbrella over my head. But when I don't, my hair frizzes up. I look like Michael Jackson before he went berserk and tried to change his race and his gender. The biggest bummer is that an umbrella makes it harder to see celebs. Not *impossible* for a trained spotter, but difficult. I look for people burrowed more deeply into their umbrellas than they need to be. Or wearing a rain hat that's pulled very low. By the time I reach Hyde Park, however, I'm damp and starving. And completely scoopless. So, I decide to wait out the rain the best way I know: lunch.

Sweet!

Cute sidewalk cafés are *everywhere*. But, I'm looking for the perfect one. Where Hugh might take Julia. Or where, say, Miley Cyrus might be sitting, reading a script. As I search, I pass white terraced houses that look scrubbed clean, flower beds bursting with sunny yellow blooms, windows with lace curtai—

OMG.

My eyes go wide.

Dark glasses. Skinny jeans. A rain hat and an alien's body. I'd recognise those freakish genetics anywhere. It's a model! Blonde hair falls down her straight back. Her legs are so long, she looks like a giraffe. Scampering closer, I recognise her immediately. It's Claudia Schiffer – that German supermodel who once went out with that freaky-looking magician. Her T-shirt is wrinkled, her ballet flats are scuffed, her lipgloss is gone. She looks amazing! Even from across the street, I can't stop staring. I try to act cool, be a New Yorker. But the celebrity reporter inside me longs to run over and ask if her fellow supermodel, Naomi Campbell, really is off her rocker. I want to tell her that I once ate at Fashion Café – the restaurant in New York City she owned with Naomi and Elle. Which, BTW, quickly fell off the runway. Who wants to eat in a restaurant owned by people who never eat? What does a model know about food?

'Miss Schiffer!' I call from across the street.

Claudia Schiffer turns, smiles, waves, then strides off on legs that are so endless I wonder if she even has a waist.

'I just saw a real model,' I say out loud. 'A *super*-model, actually.'

A Londoner walks past me and smiles nervously. Like I'm nuts. Or off my meds.

'It's okay,' I say. 'I'm a professional.'

'Notting Hill?' Francesca's lip curls with disgust. 'That neighbourhood is *so* over.'

'Not according to Claudia Schiffer,' I say.

Francesca and I are in the Red Fox pub for our end-of-the-day debriefing. It's Francesca's latest attempt to assert her bosshood. After long days of me walking everywhere and Francesca going nowhere, we meet in the pub for an update.

'Claudia Schiffer?' she scoffs. 'The model? That's your best sighting?'

'*Super*model,' I say.

'She's over thirty-five, Susan. You're reporting for a teen magazine, remember?'

'Duh,' I say. 'Claudia and I only had a brief conversation.'

Francesca takes a bite of the spinach salad with lemon juice that she calls dinner. I lick the last taste of pork chops off my lips.

'What else have you got?' she asks.

'Why do I have to tell you everything?'

'Because I'm your boss. Remember?'

Her face looks so smug I want to mush a greasy codfish all over it. I want to pour her bottle of Perrier over her head. I certainly *don't* want to tell her that my only other news of the day is the discovery of a tiny café off Portobello Road with bangers and mash to die for.

'You have spinach in your teeth,' I say.

While Francesca digs through her handbag for a mirror, I make my escape.

'See you tomorrow on the train,' I say, leaping to my feet and making a mad dash for the door.

FIFTEEN

Soon, my life in the UK settles into a comfy routine.

Early mornings: Toast and coffee with Percy and Blythe.

'Sleep well?' Percy asks every day.

'Like a rock,' I reply, 'or a cobblestone.'

Blythe says, 'We had a rowdy crowd in the pub last night. They didn't keep you awake?'

'Not at all,' I say, though I say it like a Brit: 'Not *atoll.*'

That always makes Blythe and Percy laugh.

Francesca breezes into the dining room barking, 'Tea with no sugar. Dry toast.'

No 'please'. No 'thank you'. She's such a *bee-atch*.

Late mornings: My daily commute into London feels as ordinary as a subway ride. Francesca and I rarely see each other on the way. I race to the station ahead of her. She pays extra to ride in the First Class carriage.

'I can't bear sitting with the masses any more,' she said.

Frankly, the masses and I are glad to be rid of her.

Afternoons: I've fallen in love with London. In a word, it's *awesome*. I've walked from one end of the city to the other. Though the exchange rate makes me want to cry – I can barely afford *anything* – it's fun to look in shop windows and scan menus and dream of the day I can saunter in and buy whatever I want.

I took a 'bendy' red bus once – so I could report on public transport – but it's just like any other city bus: tons of stops, tired people, kids who sit backwards and rub their sticky hands on the seats. I'd rather walk.

Like in New York, the people on the street in London are the real show. That taxi driver was right. The personality of the city seeps into your soul as you walk around. There's a unique energy here. Not frenetic, like New York. Manhattan definitely has more of an impatient edge. Like you'd better get out of the way or else. On the streets of London, I feel like I'd be politely escorted to one side if I was walking too slow. Not once do I hear a driver screech at a pedestrian, 'Get your ass in gear!'

Late afternoons: When I get back to New York, I'm definitely going to institute 'tea-time' after school.

With scones. And clotted cream, if I can find it at Zabar's.

Evenings: When it's busy at the Red Fox pub, I don a waitress apron and help out.

'Yorkshire pudding? Cottage pie?'

By now, I've eaten – devoured, really – everything Blythe cooks. It's impossible to recommend only one dish. Thank *God* for my Reeboks! If I wasn't walking several kilometres a day, I'd return to New York twice the girl I was when I left.

Nights: The most amazing transformation of all has been what I *haven't* been doing. Namely, watching television. Blythe and Percy have a telly, but I usually go up to my room after dinner or after working in the pub. I've already read the two books I brought with me. Thankfully, Ashton has a cool little bookstore and library. I can hardly believe it myself. I, Susanna Barringer, celebrity junkie, have stopped feeling like Britney and Avril and Lindsay are my imaginary friends.

Late nights: I lay my head on my soft, down-filled pillow and drift into a deep sleep. Like a cobblestone.

SIXTEEN

Ashton Library has become the link to my previous life. Once an old church, its giant oak doors lead into a large room full of books, newspapers, DVDs, magazines and a computer. With Internet access. And a fifteen-minute time limit.

'I'm on the clock.'

That's how I begin my email to Amelia. Then my hands fly across the keyboard. I tell her about Francesca's sneer, Ricky's awful mates, Blythe's Sunday roast, Claudia Schiffer's giraffe-gait.

'She was *so* nice,' I write. 'And her skin looked amazing.'

Even from across the street I could tell she has frequent professional facials.

'How r u?' I ask my best friend. 'I want details!'

I end my message the way I always do. 'Miss u madly. Luv, S.'

My email to my parents is much less specific. 'All the

street names – Pembridge Gardens, Linden Mews – sound so British! Haha.'

By the time I get to writing Ben, my time is almost up.

'I'm on the clock,' I write. Then my hands just sit there on the keys. I'm not sure what I want to say to him. I'm still so confused. I miss him, yes. But, madly? Do I wish he was here? Should I confess that I went to a pub with another boy?

'How's yr summer?' I ask, then hate myself for being so lame. Lamer still, I ask about his mom and the weather in New York (oh, *brother*). I ask if he's still skateboarding in Riverside Park (yawn). I fill my email with anything but the three words I'm not sure I feel yet. Will I ever?

'Bye,' I sign off. 'Luv, S.'

That night, the cell Francesca gave me wakes me up.

'You're in bed already?' she asks, agog.

Checking my watch, I'm embarrassed to see that it's only ten o'clock.

'No, I'm not in bed,' I lie. 'I'm reading. Literature.'

I hear loud pub sounds in the background on Francesca's end of the line. Laughter and singing. She says something, but I don't hear what it is. Not that it matters. She never says anything important, anyway.

When I don't respond, she asks, 'Well? Are you, Susan?'

No way am I telling her I have no idea what she's talking about. Not when she's at a party and I have drool on my pillow.

'Yes,' I state. 'I am.'

'You're sure?'

'Yes. I am.'

'Good.'

'Good.'

Before I can say, 'Good*bye*,' she hangs up.

I flip my pillow to the dry side, and instantly fall back asleep.

SEVENTEEN

I'm officially homesick. It happened without warning. This morning, I took a shower and washed my hair and ate toast and talked to Blythe and Percy – all with a ball of homesickness growing in my gut. Now, I'm sitting on the train, on my way into London, looking at the stunning scenery through the window, wishing I was gazing at the fire escape outside my bedroom window in New York City. I miss Amelia and Ben. I even miss the toxic waste in the Trips' pull-up nappies. At least Ricky's posse is back under some rock, and Francesca is in the front of the train.

'Paddington Station next stop.'

The full weight of my job here in London has finally dawned on me. Who am I trying to kid? I'm a *kid*. I have no idea what I'm doing. Three thousand miles across an ocean and I'm clearly a fish out of water. I've walked the streets for days, talked to teens, and soaked up the London soul. Still, I haven't a clue what to write. What made me think that I, Susanna Barringer, could snag a foreign scoop in London? I couldn't even recognise George Clooney in New York! And Francesca was right: Claudia Schiffer could be my *mother*. If my mom was ten feet tall and under a hundred pounds. Here I am in the coolest city in the world (next to my own, of course) and time is running out. I haven't even seen Buckingham Palace and already I feel like the Queen of Losers.

Beep, beep. Beep, beep.

My cell rings.

'Hello?' I say.

'Can you get into the office yourself?'

It's Francesca. I recognise the acid in her voice.

'The *Teen Scene* office?' I ask.

'No, Susan. The *post* office,' she says, sarcastically.

'Of course I can get to the office on my own,' I say. Though it's not entirely true. Unbelievably, I've never actually been inside the *Scene* magazine offices in London. I've been hoofing it all over town, searching for my scoop. But I did drop Francesca off there once and I do have the address. Unlike New York taxi drivers, London cabbies are legendary for knowing how to get anywhere, right? All I have to do is hop in and tell him where I want to go. Right?

'No prob,' I say, swallowing.

'Good,' Francesca says. 'I have an, um, errand to run. But I'll be there before the big meeting.'

'What big meeting?' I ask.

'Very funny, Sue.'

Then she hangs up.

The barfy lump in my stomach gets bigger.

Today's London cabbie is every bit the expert my previous cabbie was. He chats, he laughs, he turns onto narrow one-way streets with the ease of an Indie car driver. Almost before I settle in for the ride, we're there.

'Have you been to Westminster Abbey?' he asks me, as I fumble with the pounds in my dollar-sized wallet.

'Not yet,' I say.

'The skateboarders are awesome.'

'Skateboarders? In the church where Henry the Eighth was crowned? Don't you go to hell for that?'

He laughs. 'Not *inside* the Abbey. In front of it.'

'Ah.' I pay my fare, plus a huge tip that I can barely afford. No, I say to myself, I am *not* a black hole from Kansas.

'You have to catch them before the coppers make them move on.'

'Cool,' I say. 'Thanks for the tip.'

'Same to you.'

As the cab idles in front of *Scene*'s London office, I hop out. Then I take a deep breath and march into the office building where God-knows-what is waiting for me.

EIGHTEEN

'Susanna!'

My head whips around.

'That's your name, right?'

'Right.'

'How lovely to meet you! Welcome. I'm Delia. The editor-in-chief here. Nell has told me so much about you. Can I get you some coffee?'

I blink. Then I look down to make sure I'm not still in my pyjamas. Not only did Delia get my name right on the first try, but she's totally nice, too. Her brown hair is short – almost a boy-cut. Her skin is freckled, her hips actually belong to a woman, and – most surprising – she's American. Well, let me take that back. The *most* surprising thing about my London boss is that she offered to get *me* coffee. Am I in a parallel universe? Am I being punk'd?

'The meeting will start in a few minutes,' Delia says. 'Make yourself comfortable in the conference room.'

I walk into the conference room, sit down and take out my notepad and pen. Whatever this meeting is about, I, Susanna Barringer, will be prepared for it.

The conference room is huge – the kind of space you see on a television lawyer show. One wall is all glass, the other, all windows. We're on the top floor, high enough to feel like we're floating. A giant oval table in the centre of the room looks like a visiting spaceship.

I'm all alone at first. But staff members eventually file in, most carrying coffee or tea. They chatter with one another, say hi to me. Everyone is so nice. Not a Francesca in the bunch!

'Good morning, all. Cheers.'

Delia enters breezily and sits at one end of the large table. She says, 'Let's get this show on the road.'

My nerves return in a flash flood. Is Francesca expecting me to cover for her? Is that what she said on the phone last night? Where did she say she was going this morning? Some kind of errand?

'Susanna?' Delia says.

Both eyes fly open.

'Uh,' I sputter, 'Francesca will be—'

At that exact moment, Francesca bustles in.

'Sorry I'm late,' she says, breathless.

99

I exhale audibly. Francesca squeezes a chair in next to mine and sits. Her cheeks are pink and her hair is mussed up. Her lipstick looks funny, too. Thank goodness she's here to cover for herself.

Delia repeats, 'Susanna?'

'Here,' I say.

The staff laughs. She says to me, 'Ready when you are.'

'Ready for what?'

Again, the entire staff chuckles. Francesca glares at me and whispers, 'Stand up.'

Stand? Francesca elbows me and I stand, even more wobbly on my Frankenstein's monster shoes than I was on the cobblestone streets of Ashton. All of a sudden, the bright sunlight from the wall of windows burns my face. My heart is going berserk. My chest actually *hurts* because of the thumping. Can a ventricle get bruised? I wonder. Can a teenager's heart pump so furiously that it explodes? And, most importantly, is there any possibility that some of this surging blood might nourish enough brain cells to help me figure out what I'm supposed to be doing?

'Just fill us in on your progress so far, Susanna,' Delia says. 'What's your angle for the *American Teen in London* piece?'

OMG. *That.*

I swallow. Or try to. My mouth is so dry I gulp only hot air. Why, oh why, didn't I say yes to Delia's offer of coffee!? At the very least, I could have bought some time and sympathy by burning my throat.

'Well,' I begin, consuming another mouthful of hot air. 'I, uh, there's just, um, so much—'

'The basics will be fine,' Delia says.

I look around the table. All eyes are on me. Cells are on vibrate. BlackBerrys are off. Mugs of tea sit steaming. My head feels like it's filled with helium. I'm grateful for the muscles in my neck that keep my skull from floating up to the ceiling. What am I doing here? I'm a kid! I'm a fraud! I'm a virgin who dresses like a waiter!

'Urban pirates,' I blurt out, gripping the edge of the table with both hands.

'Urban pirates?' Delia echoes. 'Hmm. I'm intrigued. Go on.'

Go on? I have no idea why I even said that! Desperately, I summon all the powers of the universe to implant an idea in my empty swirling brain. When nothing arrives, I beg. Still zippo. Dead air. Then I flash on Keith Franklin – the hot photog from *Scene* magazine – the guy who taught me to act *as if*.

'Act like you belong,' he once told me, 'and everyone will believe that you do.'

So, I do. I act. I confidently dive in even though there's every chance I'll sink as quickly as a cobblestone thrown off London Bridge.

'My article is a juxtaposition of two sets of urban pirates,' I state. 'London teens versus New York. Sort of a mock battle between kids who live in the two best cities in the world. What unites us, what divides us. Topshop, skateboarding at Westminster Abbey, pints at the local pub, soccer . . . Kate Moss versus, um, Heidi Klum. Leona Lewis versus Jordin Sparks. I'll cover it all. From fish to chips.'

The staff laugh. Delia beams. Emboldened, I go on.

'The angle will be *my* angle. My point of view. A real teen. Not some twenty-something editorial assistant pretending she's still in school.'

Brazenly, I glance down at Francesca. I'm stunned to see a love bite on her neck. Was that her *errand*? An early-morning make-out session? Did she meet some guy on the train?

'Sluts versus good girls,' I continue. 'Celebrities versus stars, royalty v class, Amy v Britney – I'll cover it all. As *me*. Susanna Barringer. An American teen in London.'

The room bursts into applause.

'Now *that's* a reporter,' Delia says. 'Bravo, Susanna!'

I beam. Feel the love wash over me.

'That's about all I have for now,' I say.

'Brilliant!' Delia says.

Regally, I sit back in my chair and feel a wave of *relief* wash over me. I did it. I made it through the mystery meeting. Thank you, Keith! Francesca looks relieved, too. I guess my work is a reflection on her, too. I pleased my mini-boss and my maxi-boss. Nell will be happy. Francesca will leave me alone. And Delia will eagerly await my unique view of the teen scene in London. It's true – I, Susanna Barringer, am an awesome reporter!

As the meeting continues onto other business, my grin slowly morphs into a grimace. My confidence dribbles out of the bottom of my feet. That lump of dread in my gut is now the size of a basketball. Or, I should say, a football, aka a soccer ball. I've felt a lump this size before. I had it in the limo on the way to Randall Sanders's movie premiere, after my walk down the red carpet on Oscar night, and backstage at Fashion Week. I'm quite familiar with this sensation of wanting to hurl: now that I've told everyone what I plan to do, how the hell am I going to do it?

NINETEEN

'Is that what I think it is?'

That's what I ask Francesca, flat out, about the lip-shaped red mark on her neck.

She doesn't answer me. Instead, she smoothes a clump of her hair over the right side of her neck.

'The train conductor?' I ask, agog. 'The guy pushing the coffee cart down the aisle? Who gave you that hickey?'

She says, 'None of your beeswax,' and disappears into the sea of ringing cell phones at the London office of *Scene* magazine.

Oh well. I have bigger things on my mind than the love bite on Francesca's neck. I have to uncover all the differences between teens in London and New York.

I gulp.

Checking my handbag to make sure my cell is turned on, I confidently march through the office with no idea what I'm going to do next.

'Good job, Susanna.' Delia pops out of a doorway to give me a hug.

Good job? I nearly faint. And a *hug*? I've been in England less than a month and my overseas boss has already praised me more than Nell ever did. Well, almost more. There was that one time Nell said, 'We're very proud of you here.' Though she was quick to add, 'Before you leave, Sue, pick me up a mango smoothie at Jamba Juice.'

Here, in London, the land of lords and ladies and a Fergie who is a real Duchess, I'm treated like a princess!

'I won't let you down,' I say to Delia, hugging her back.

'Better not!' she chirps. Then she goes back to work.

Again, I gulp.

As I walk through the London office, I feel the same buzz I felt in New York. Laptop keys are clicking, various ringtones chime through the air, bits of conversation tickle my ears.

'Is Lily Allen's fave food still beans and cheese on toast?'

'Whose photo is first on the "Hot Scots" piece? McAvoy or McGregor?'

'Can anyone confirm that Amy Winehouse has a new tat?'

Wow. I can't believe I'm here. In London. Hot on a new scoop. Ready to take the world by stor—

'One more thing, Susanna.' Delia suddenly appears behind me. 'I'll need a first draft of "Urban Pirates" by next week, okay?'

'*Next* week?'

'Is that a problem?'

Problem? I say to myself. More like Mission *Impossible*. Out of the question. Are you nuts? No way, no how.

'No worries,' I say, brightly. 'I'm on it.'

'That's our girl,' Delia says.

Then she leaves me to dash for the elevator before the lump in my stomach reminds me how far I'm in over my head.

Today is sunny in a hazy way. The sidewalk is still filled with upturned faces, but there's a sense of desperation about them. Like everyone knows the sun is on its way out. As I walk, I think about how the very same sun shines such a different colour on various parts of the world. In Hollywood, it's lemon yellow. In New York, it's saffron. In London, it's more like ivory. What colour is the sun in Africa, I wonder? Sandy brown? Amber?

'Susanna!'

Wheeling around, I come face-to-face with a bouquet of wildflowers. My eyes bug out of my head. Behind the flowers, it's *Ricky*. From Ashton. The blond tips of his spiky hair poke up over the drooping blossoms.

'What are you doing here?' I ask. 'How did you find me?'

Ricky pushes the flowers closer to my face and looks down at his trainers. 'The only thing that matters are these,' he says. 'If we can start over, take the flowers. If you can't forgive me for my rude mates, walk away and I'll eat these flowers for lunch.'

I'm tempted to turn and stomp off. But Ricky's cute face looks so hopeful as he peers around the bouquet. And there's that goofy lopsided grin.

'Dad gave me the entire day off so I could show you around London.'

I sigh.

He says, 'London, *England*. Not London, Ohio. You'll love it.'

'There's a London in Ohio?'

'And one in Kentucky and Texas, too. Don't they teach you anything in New York?'

Now I chuckle. Ricky's grin is contagious. You can't

107

look at it without feeling giddy. A tour of London with a smile like that? How can I resist?

'I'm working today,' I say.

'On what?'

'The differences between teens in New York and London.'

'So, you're planning to just wander the streets in the hopes of stumbling over a story?'

'No,' I say, scoffing. Then I think, 'Well, yeah. That's what I've been doing since I got here.'

Ricky thrusts the flowers at me. 'Wouldn't you rather have a real Englishman as your tour guide?'

He has a point. He also smells slightly of hay and burning wood. It's delicious. His eyes are all sparkly, like there's a blazing fire inside his head. I feel my cheeks get pink. My resolve weakens. Why blame a boy for his stupid friends? He's not responsible for them. Is Ricky the boy I've been waiting for? My rock star?

'C'mon, Susanna,' he says, softly.

I take the bouquet and lift it to my nose. The flowers have no scent, they're not sunflowers (my favourite) and they're ragged and wilted as if Ricky picked them in a field in Ashton – which he probably did. Still, my heart melts.

'Your friends are jerks,' I say.

'It doesn't mean I am,' Ricky says.

I sigh again. He can see that I'm softening.

'Follow me,' he says gently.

'Where are we going?' I ask.

'Down,' he says, taking my hand and tossing the flowers in the trash. Then he pulls me towards London's massive subway system. Finally, I'm going to ride the Tube.

'Okay, Ricky. But, remember, I'm working.'

He laughs. I barely believe it myself.

This is one dangerous boy, I think. A boy like this can make a girl like me do almost anything.

A native New Yorker such as myself would never admit to wanting to see London as a tourist. That's for Texans, or Iowans. Or black holes from Kansas. Not for a girl who walked the red carpet and infiltrated the backstage scene at Fashion Week. But, as Ricky and I weave through the sidewalk crowd towards the underground, I'm dying to ask him if we can see London Bridge, Buckingham Palace, Big Ben, Abbey Road – all the places I have yet to visit. Don't London teens ever hang out at tourist traps? My friends and I spend time in Times Square!

'Westminster Abbey,' I blurt out.

'What about it?'

'I need to see the skateboarders before the coppers chase them away.'

Ricky rolls his eyes.

'Work,' I say. 'Remember?'

Reluctantly, Ricky agrees. Like a true gentleman, he even buys me an Oyster card in the Tube station. My heart softens. I'm glad I gave him a second chance. Clearly he's a nice boy after all.

We begin our descent. Down, down, down – we go so far underground I can't believe we don't hit China. If you ask me, the Tube should be called, 'The Escalator to Hell'. Not that it's dirty or flaming or anything. Just the opposite. London's subway system looks cleaner than New York's. Very high-tech, too. TV monitors mounted to the wall flash ads at us as we sink lower and lower underground. It's just that I've never been this far below the surface of the Earth before. If Hell is anywhere, it's got to be down here.

I follow Ricky and the crowds to a train platform that's just like ours back home. But, when the train arrives, I spot more differences. The seats – like the train to Ashton – are cushioned. The subway car feels like a long, narrow living room full of indifferent guests. Like New York, no one looks anyone else in the eye. Unlike New York, tons of discarded newspapers litter the seats.

'Recycling?' I ask Ricky.

He nods. 'You never have to buy the morning paper if you take the Tube to work.'

It only takes a few minutes to get to the Westminster stop. As Ricky and I rise up from the underground, I have the weird sensation that I'm stepping back in time. I half expect to see Queen Victoria stroll by in one of those wedding cake gowns. I can almost hear the clopping of horse hooves on the cobblestones. Right in front of us, there it is: the awesome gothic church, Westminster Abbey. Where Elton John sang his sad song for Diana. The stone is bright white in the sunlight. And the tops of the spires are all spiky, like Ricky's hair. It's truly spectacular. And totally bizarre. In front, there's a line of protesters against Scientology and, yes, skateboarders. They've set up a ramp and are flipping, twirling, falling.

'Ouch,' I say, wincing, as one of the skateboarders wipes out.

'Seen enough?' Ricky asks, impatient.

I look up at the Abbey.

'What's the rush? While we're here, how can we not go inside?'

Ricky groans. But he follows me into the church.

The interior of Westminster Abbey looks like a giant rib cage. The sky-high arched ceiling is held up by beautiful curved stone beams. The side windows are all delicate stained glass. It's an impossible structure. How could this airy space support a stone roof? I walk down a side aisle, my mouth open, taking in all the beauty.

'Seen enough?' Ricky asks again.

'How can you ever see enough of a church like this?' I answer.

He heads for the exit. I guess it's like the Statue of Liberty, I say to myself. It's awesome unless you see it everyday. Then, it's as ordinary as Zabar's. How many times have I walked right past Saint Patrick's Cathedral on Fifth Avenue on my way to H&M?

'C'mon, Susanna,' Ricky says.

And off we go, on our whirlwind tour.

Ricky doesn't seem like a country boy at all. He walks at a half-run – the typical city pace. He weaves through crowded sidewalks like a pro. Not that I can't keep up. Even though I'm wearing my four-inch Payless platforms today, I'm able to maintain the pace as any native New Yorker could.

'Which bridge is this?' I ask, as we race-walk across the Thames.

'Westminster,' Ricky replies. Which, of course, makes perfect sense.

The water in the Thames is greenish-grey and flickering with tiny whitecaps. It's much narrower than the Hudson. Once again, I'm dumbstruck by the history of it. I'm walking over water that Henry the Eighth sailed on! How cool is that?

'This is where I hang out when I come to the city,' Ricky says on the other side of the bridge. 'The South Bank.'

Ricky's demeanour instantly changes on the south side of the Thames. He walks more slowly, bobs his head. He checks everyone out.

I look around, too. Frankly, I'm not that impressed. Though there are a couple of enticing museums – modern art and a *movieum* full of British films – much of the South Bank looks like Coney Island. There are even hot dog stands! Plus, ice-cream vendors and – ugh – a Mackey D's. In the land of fish and chips, why would anyone eat a Big Mac?

The kids look rough. Their eyes are all bloodshot. They make me nervous. This is Ricky's local hangout?

As we walk along the river, the South Bank becomes more and more like New York City's South Street Seaport. Or like the piazza in Covent Garden. There are hip-hop dancers, musicians and living statues performing for the tourists . . . like me.

'The London Eye!' I shriek.

There it is. One of the tourist traps I've been dying to see. Admittedly, riding London's giant Ferris wheel is about as lame as having your photo taken trying to get one of the Queen's guards to laugh. It's the British equivalent of New York City's boat trip around Manhattan. But, how cool will it be to see London from above?

Amazingly, Ricky doesn't groan or roll his eyes. He seems eager to hop on the Eye.

'It's on me,' I say, at the ticket office. Thank goodness there's no line. Before he can protest, we get right on, and slowly rise up.

Okay, I'm not proud of this – being a New Yorker and all. But, I *love* riding the London Eye. (I also love the Circle Line tour boat around Manhattan, but don't tell anyone.) Ricky and I are in an enclosed glass capsule all to ourselves. The wheel turns very slowly and, as we rise up, the whole of London stretches out before us.

'What's that?' I ask.

'Scotland Yard.'

'And that?'

114

'Parliament.'

'And way down there?'

'The Tower of London.'

London is a gorgeous city – on land as well as in the air. It's the perfect mixture of old and new. Scotland Yard looks like a building made of Lego. Parliament looks like it's made of sand. Even though I feel a twinge of guilt for riding a Ferris wheel when I should be researching my Urban Pirates piece, I tell myself that I *am* working. I'm absorbing London through the combined eyes of a New York girl and an Ashton boy.

'That's Big Ben, right?' I ask, pointing. 'How do they change the clock for daylight-saving time? Do you even *have* daylight-saving time here?'

Ricky is silent. Suddenly, I notice that he's looking at me more intensely than he's looking at London. His light green eyes are dark. He no longer grins.

'I read that you can see Windsor Castle on a clear day,' I splutter.

'Your hair smells like pineapple,' he whispers.

It's passion fruit, actually, but no way am I going to correct him. Not when he's looking at me like that.

Ricky takes a step closer to me and inhales. My heart leaps into my throat. I'm freaking out a little. Here I am, up in the air, with a boy I barely know. An older boy. What was I thinking? It'll take a good twenty more minutes for us to revolve our way back to Earth.

'Is *that* Windsor Castle?' I squeak, pointing off in the distance.

Ricky buries his face in my curls and I freeze. He presses his body against mine and a tiny moan escapes his lips. My eyes pop open. My heart pounds so hard I swear I feel the glass capsule sway with each beat.

'Have you ever been to Stonehenge?' I ask, gulping air. 'I did an oral report on it last year in World History class. It's awesome. If you've never been, it's totally wort—'

His lips pressed against my ear, Ricky repeats the words, 'Oral report.'

'Is it a sundial?' I say, frantically. 'A temple to the gods? A giant stone crop circle? We'll never know!'

Ricky whispers something into my hair. I don't hear it, but I *feel* it – his warm breath makes me shiver. Unable to control myself, I blather on about aliens and prehistoric visitations and why would anyone go to all that trouble unless it was a matter of life and dea –

To shut me up, Ricky lands a kiss on my lips. Hard. An alien landing. A British invasion. He kisses me too hard, really. We even bump teeth. He must think my mouth is bigger than it is. (Not that I blame him with all that nervous chatter.) Ricky seems to be kissing my lower nose and upper chin more than my lips. He's slobbering all over my face. Honestly, my first reaction to this first kiss is, 'Ewww.'

'Susanna,' he whispers when he comes up for air.

'That's me,' I say, like a total tool.

Before I can stop him, Ricky is back on my lips. *Over* my lips, I should say. His tongue is now searching for my vocal cords. How long is this ride? What kind of stupid Ferris wheel takes half an hour to rotate once?

As if reading my mind, Ricky pulls away from my lips and says, 'We have time.'

'Time?' I echo. 'Time to swing by Buckingham Palace?'

He doesn't answer. Not that I blame him. Even as I said it, I knew it was lame. But my brain is buzzing and I'm suddenly questioning the mechanics of the London Eye. What, exactly, is holding this capsule onto the wheel? Do they have safety inspectors in England? Doesn't all this rainy weather make things rusty?

Ricky moans again. He pushes away my passion-fruited hair and lunges for my neck. I feel like I'm being attacked by a blowfish. He's nibbling and sucking and, frankly, freaking me out.

'My carotid artery,' I say. 'Careful.'

I've seen enough horror movies to know what can happen if the big vein in your neck is punctured. This glass capsule would turn red in an instant.

Ricky's lips release the skin on my neck with a *pop!* He mumbles, 'I love American girls.'

Clearly out of my mind, I flash on an old Beach Boys song.

East Coast girls are hip, I really dig the clothes they wear . . .

Ricky returns to my neck, whispering, 'And New York girls are the hottest.'

Can't wait to get back to the States, back to the cutest girls in the worl—

'Hey, wait a minute!' I say.

Ricky continues making a meal out of my neck.

'American *girls*. Plural?'

My brain suddenly kicks into gear. The smeared lipstick. Mussed hair. Bright red love bite.

'Were you on the train with Francesca this morning?' I ask, incredulous.

'What does that matter?' he says.

'Did you ride with her in the first-class carriage?'

He shrugs. 'Briefly,' he says.

'Is this a . . . a . . . *twofer?*'

'Huh?'

'Get off my neck!'

I push Ricky back. The sound of his lips releasing my skin is like a champagne cork on New Year's Eve. The glass capsule rocks.

'Was this your plan all along? Getting me up in the air?'

'Relax, Susanna,' he whispers.

'You think you can just make out with every American girl who lands in Ashton?' I ask, indignant.

Ricky smirks. 'I've seen *The Bachelor* and *Girls Gone Wild*. I spent my sixth form in America. I know what American girls are like.'

My jaw falls to the floor. I toss my hair and wipe Ricky's slobber off my neck with my sleeve.

'I don't care what you did with Francesca this morning. Did you give her wildflowers, too? The same bouquet? Is that why they were so limp?'

Ricky glances down at the Thames.

'I bought you an Oyster card,' he says.

'So?'

'You owe me.'

Now my blood boils. I fumble through my handbag for a few pounds to throw in his face.

'You must be a virgin,' he says with a sneer.

Suddenly, Ricky's spiked hair looks ridiculous. The

silver in his diamond stud earrings looks cheap and tarnished. How could I ever have thought he was cute?

'You may think American girls are all like Francesca or those reality show skanks,' I say. 'But I, Susanna Barringer, am nothing like those other girls. If I was on *The Bachelor*, I'd tell that conceited jerk to take his rose and cram it up his—'

I stop.

'I'm not going to say anything more. I'm a *lady*.'

Ricky crosses his arms in front of his chest and turns his back on me.

All I can think is, *when is this bloody ride ever going to end!?*

TWENTY

The moment the London Eye touches ground, I'm off and running.

'Susanna, wait!'

Ricky calls after me, but no way am I going to turn around. Ever. My platforms fly across the pavement. I can't wait to cross back over the Thames and leave Ricky behind with his South Bank thugs.

'How stupid can you be?' I ask myself. Of course you can judge a boy by his friends! Who would have such jerky friends unless they, too, were a jerk?

Friends.

As soon as my heart stops flinging itself against my breastbone, my mind flashes on Amelia and Ben. I'd give anything to have them here with me now. *Both* of them.

Now, my heart *sinks*. How could I ever have thought I wanted someone more exciting than Ben? More like Ricky – a guy who's just looking for an easy mark like

Francesca. A boy who thinks real girls are like the fake idiots they see on TV.

I hang my head. I've been so stupid. I feel like Dorothy in *The Wizard of Oz*. True love has been in my own backyard, but I was too blind to see it.

Mentally, I pummel myself all the way across Westminster Bridge, past Big Ben and the skateboarders in front of the Abbey. Ricky stopped following me ages ago, but I can't stop fleeing. I feel humiliated. How could I think an older boy like that would go for a girl like me? How gullible could I be?

I walk ... and walk. Until I calm down. Till my pulse rate returns to normal. I trawl the London streets in the warmth of the late-morning sun until I'm sure of my next move. It takes almost an hour, though I've known it all along.

'Do you know where I can find an Internet café?' I ask a girl on the sidewalk.

'Hmmm.' She thinks for a moment, then points down a side street. 'You ought to find one around there,' she says.

Thanking her, I take off again. The Thames is behind me; all of glorious London – and the rest of my life – is ahead. It doesn't take long to find what I'm looking for: a connection. A *real* connection. I order a skinny latte and sit in front of the blank computer screen. My heart starts pounding again. My ears buzz. But now, the haze has cleared. In the middle of London, surrounded by so much history, I see my future. I, Susanna Barringer, have finally, fully, properly fallen in love. With *Ben.* The boy (almost) next door.

TWENTY-ONE

'It's me,' I write. Then I wait to see if Ben is online. He's not. Not that I'm surprised. It's just past dawn in New York.

'I miss u sooooo much,' I continue. 'London is truly amazing. Wish u were here.'

That phrase – such a cliché – has never felt more real. I want to show Ben the inside of Westminster Abbey, the outside of Ashton, the overview of London from the sky. I want him to smell the passion fruit in my hair. I want to tell him everything. I want to start over.

'I'll check in l8r,' I write. 'Luv, S.'

Then, I delete the last four letters.

'I love you,' I type instead. Three words that suddenly, amazingly, feel exactly right.

I know I'm supposed to be working. I know this isn't a day off. But, who can work when they're in love?

How can you concentrate when it's the most beautiful day ever?

I keep walking on the sunny side of the street. Even though it's really the hazy side. After a while, it looks like I've stumbled upon the Park Avenue of London. Along a beautiful green lawn, with old trees and new grass, there's one awesome townhouse after another. Maybe they're houses, I think. Whatever they are, it's clear that rich people live in them. Then again, it's probably more like Fifth Avenue in New York. *Uber* rich abodes, but on a public park. So it's probably noisy on the weekend.

Practically skipping along the walkway, I think about Amelia. I was going to email her, too, but I decided to wait. Don't ask me why, but I feel like keeping my love for Ben all to myself. For a little while, at least. Maybe it's because Mel is so practical and sensible. No doubt, she'll question my sincerity.

'You sure this isn't just a reaction to the suckfest on the London Eye?' she'll ask me.

'I'm sure,' I'll say.

But, I won't know how to explain how I know for sure. I just know. Yeah, Ricky was the catalyst. But he only showed me what I already knew, deep down. Ricky took my blinkers off.

'You sure this isn't just a case of absence making the heart grow fonder?' Mel will ask.

'I'm sure,' I'll say.

'You sure Ben is the *one*?' Mel will ask, finally.

I'll chuckle and say, '*I'm* not sure, but my heart is.'

And then she'll know. For sure.

Suddenly, as spectacular as a rose bursting open, I see a sight that takes my breath away. OMG! It's Buckingham Palace. Right there! Sitting at the end of the park, behind a gold-tipped wrought iron fence, the Queen's gargantuan mansion rises up before my eyes. No offence to our president, but the Queen's palace makes the White House look like a B&B. You could get a good workout jogging from one end to the other. I'd hate to be the royal maid!

A huge crowd is gathered in the round plaza across from the Queen's house, and in front of her ornate gates. A giant golden statue of Queen Victoria shimmers in the sunlight. Two large beds of red flowers make me happy just to look at them. It's all a postcard come alive, though without any shade it's jammed full of sweaty people. You can't walk a metre without stepping into somebody's photograph. I glance at the top of the building to see which flag is flying.

'She's home!' I squeal.

Thanks to World History class, I learned that the Queen's own flag – a yellow, maroon and blue banner called the Royal Standard – flies above Buckingham Palace whenever the Queen is inside. I wonder where the corgis are. Chewing on their royal rawhide bones? Do they have their own canine quarters?

At that moment, I hear drums beating in the distance. Horns blaring, too. They are faint at first. Then the marching band gets louder. Horses *clip clop* on the pavement. All eyes face the long strip of road on the other side of the park. I wiggle as far as I can to the front of the crowd. The first thing I see is a tall, furry hat bobbing up and down. Then several flashes of red. Then I can't believe my eyes. It's the changing of the guard! Right here, right now. And I'm in the middle of an age-old British tradition. How lucky can an American girl get?

The first batch of the Queen's guards arrives on horseback, the rest march on foot. They all wear the red jacket, white belt and black trousers that are so familiar. And, of course, that humungous furry hat with the gold chin strap. Man! Their heads must be boiling hot! Though you'd never know any of the guards felt uncomfortable. They all look deadly serious. Like the Queen really needs protecting even though she's probably in her royal backyard playing with her dogs.

'This is awesome,' I say to a fellow gawker, as the entire spectacle enters the open gates of Buckingham Palace. 'Why would anyone want to end the monarchy?'

'Because it costs us forty million pounds a year!' someone in the crowd shouts.

I do a quick calculation in my mind and I see his point. Would I want to pay eighty million dollars a year to see a marching band and (rarely) a Queen who waves a gloved hand at her 'subjects' and knights old rock stars with swords? Hmmm.

Still, at this moment, I'm thrilled to see the show. The only thing even close to this in the US is the changing of the guard at the Tomb of the Unknown Soldier in Washington. My parents took me to DC when I was a kid. All I remember thinking was, 'Why do they need to guard a dead guy? Where do they think he's going?'

By the time the guards are beyond the Queen's gates, however, I begin to wonder what the fuss is all about. No one can see anything, yet the crowds remain. The marching band music is so faint, it's barely audible. Tourists hold their phones up to take a picture, but what are they shooting? The back of another tourist's head?

The whole spectacle gets me thinking. Are tourist hotspots just an example of mass hysteria? I need to see what's going on simply because everyone else is? Are humans really just followers after all? Or is it our need to belong? Be part of a group? Is that why so many tourists in New York flock to the World Trade Centre location? It's now a fenced-in construction site, but hundreds of people still head downtown to see the big hole. Do we all need to feel like we're part of something?

While I mull over these cosmic questions, I realise – once again – that I'm starving. OMG! Who knew how draining it could be to make sure the Queen and her corgis are safe behind a closed gate? Thankfully, Francesca (aka Skankarella) hasn't called me. Even though I haven't worked much today, I still deserve a lunch break! But, as I look around, I don't see many interesting places to eat. I want something unique, something local. I want to dine with the English, not a bunch of Americans.

As the crowd dissolves into London, I ask a police officer – I mean, *copper* – where I can get a great British lunch.

'Got a tube pass?' he asks me.

'Yes.' Like the honking red hickey on my neck, I still have the Oyster card Ricky bought me.

'Hop on the tube to London Bridge station and ask someone to point you in the direction of Borough Market.'

'A market?' I ask.

'It's an outdoor food court – it's only open a few days a week, but today's one of them. Trust me. You'll love it.'

I trust him. What have I got to lose?

TWENTY-TWO

The copper is totally right. Borough Market is mind-blowing. It's like walking into a giant train station full of food. Like Covent Garden on steroids. Butchers sell fresh meat, farmers offer every vegetable known to man, and chefs all over the market cook up dishes that smell so good your mouth waters the moment you walk beneath the huge arched entrance. There's so much to choose from, it's impossible to decide what to eat. I stroll all over the market – under the glass roof, outside into the sun – looking for the ideal local dish.

'Razor clams?' one vendor suggests.

No.

'Black pudding?' suggests another.

Nah.

'Chip Buttie?'

Chip Buttie? I'm intrigued. 'What is it?' I ask.

A woman in a white apron answers, 'A sandwich.'

I love sandwiches!

'No pig's blood, I hope.'

'Nope.' She laughs. 'It's vegetarian.'

A Chip Buttie it is, then. Why not try something healthy?

The woman turns to her stove and I can't believe my eyes. She takes two large pieces of bread, slathers butter on them, and puts them facedown on the hot grill. While they sizzle, she dunks a basket full of fries into boiling oil. When the fries are cooked, my chef salts them, then – get this – puts the fries between the two pieces of buttered, grilled bread, cuts it and serves it to me. That's a Chip Buttie. A French fry sandwich!

I bite into the warm, soft, buttery sandwich and feel the oil and salt dance over my tongue. It's *delicious*. Way better than the chips Ricky's dad served.

'I think I just became a vegetarian,' I say.

The chef grins and says, 'Cheers.'

It takes me all of two minutes to devour my French fry sandwich. My lips glisten with grease. I order a diet soda to wash it all down and that makes the chef laugh again.

'Diet?' she asks.

I see her point. What's a hundred more calories when I just ate a grilled French fry sandwich? Still.

With the excitement of the day fading from my

mind, and my Chip Buttie and diet soda settling in my stomach, I suddenly feel incredibly sleepy. I long to lie down on a bench and take a nap. I want another warm Chip Buttie to use as a pillow. Instead, I rub the feeling back into my face and head straight for the Tube station. Somehow, I'll figure out which train to take to the station. I've had a full day. It's time to go home – to Ashton and the Red Fox pub and my narrow bed with the puffy *real* pillow just waiting for my head.

I awake with the taste of butter still on my lips. Unbelievably, I slept straight through the night, in my clothes. My mascara feels like Superglue. The underwire on my bra is digging into my ribs. It's barely morning. My whole body feels as though it's covered in soot.

'I'm in love!' I say to the rising sun.

Everything – the ride on the London Eye, Ricky's love bite, Francesca's sneer, my looming deadline – is cloudy compared to the one clear vision in my head: Ben. He's the *one*. He's *always* been the one.

'What an awesome day!'

I get up, shower, dress and skip downstairs to make myself toast and coffee. Percy is up; Blythe and Francesca aren't.

'You're alive,' Percy says.

Laughing, I reply, 'I've never been *more* alive.'

'We knocked on your door last night to see if you wanted supper, and you said you'd be right down. Ten hours later, here you are.'

'Sorry,' I say. 'A Chip Buttie did me in.'

Percy nods. 'You're not the first.'

Sipping my steaming coffee, I sink back in my chair and smile. How lucky am I? A free trip to London, an article in the first issue of *Teen Scene* and a boy waiting for me at home. At least I *hope* Ben is waiting for me.

'Is the village library open yet?' I ask Percy.

He looks at his watch. 'About half an hour.'

'Brilliant!'

I finish my breakfast as the morning sunlight streams through the pub windows. The stuffed fox in the corner seems to be grinning instead of snarling. His auburn coat looks almost pettable. And the aroma of my coffee is so yummy I want to dab some behind my ears. It's one of those mornings that makes you feel sad for the people who are still asleep.

'Off to London today?' Percy asks.

'Yes. But first, I have something important to take care of in New York.'

TWENTY-THREE

Ashton would be beautiful in a hailstorm, but today, with the white-yellow sun illuminating the pale orange stone buildings, it's impossibly picturesque. Like a white horse pulling a red carriage through the first snow in Central Park, it makes you happy just to see it.

I'm the first person in the library.

'Beautiful morning,' the librarian says.

'The best,' I reply.

I log on. Before anything else, I read the email from my mom. It makes me laugh.

'Henry and Sam have entered a "tantrum" phase,' she writes about my little brothers. 'Evan is the peacemaker. Yesterday, he sent both of them to the naughty bench.'

Mom tells me that Dad is on an interesting forensics case – a floating body from the Hudson – and that she needs to colour her hair more often since I left.

'Don't forget to look left when you cross a London

street,' she writes, signing her message, 'Love from your old grey-haired mum.'

I hit the 'reply' button and select an emoticon that's laughing hysterically. Emoticons are too lame to use with my friends, but Mom thinks they're cute.

'Sounds like Evan is the Terminator more than the peacemaker,' I write. 'I'm looking left, right and up. I miss all of you. The Queen says hi.'

Next, I send Mel an instant message.

'You up?' I ask.

No answer. Not that I'm surprised. It's the middle of the night back in New York.

'Oh, Mel,' I write. 'I've been such a dunce.'

For the next few minutes, my fingers fly. I tell my best friend everything. I answer all her questions before she even asks them. At the end, I exhale and ask, 'Any ivies lower their tuition for you yet? Haha.'

An older woman in a powder blue cardigan walks through the library's front door.

'Do you need the computer?' I ask her.

'Goodness, no,' she says. 'I have a laptop.'

I chuckle. Then I hit 'send' and get ready to open the email I've been dying to see. The subject line reads: 'Big Ben'. My Ben. The boy I've loved all along but didn't know it.

My heart thuds as I click on his name. I expect to see a long message about his summer – how stinky and steamy the city is, how he's already getting notices about the new school year, how his mom wants to buy one of those yappy, shivering Paris Hilton dogs. But, when I open Ben's email, my pounding heart skips a full beat. In a giant font size, boldface, are four little words. Words I'm now dying to hear.

'I luv u 2.'

Who needs to say anything more?

TWENTY-FOUR

I smile all day. On the train into London. As I wander around the city absorbing the teen scene. As I tilt my face up to the sky.

I smile all week. As one day blends into the next. As I scope out Camden Market – the outdoor maze of tiny shops that reek of incense and ethnic food – where cool Urban Pirates shop. As I watch more skateboarders fly through the air in Trafalgar Square. As I check out the other 'circus' in London – Piccadilly. It reminds me of Times Square at home, only less wattage. Again, I see London the way you should see New York – on foot. I cross what I thought was the famous London Bridge (though it's actually Tower Bridge) and stroll over the famed intersection on Abbey Road. I fantasise about living with Ben in Notting Hill and shopping for books with him on Charing Cross Road. I span London from Charles Dickens's East End to Andrew Lloyd Webber's West

End. Smiling all the way. Even on my daily call from Francesca.

'Where are you?' she asks, instead of saying, 'Hello.'

'Around,' I reply.

'You have a deadline, you know.'

'I know.'

'Is your article almost done?'

'Almost,' I say.

'God, Susanna. You're so obstreperous.'

'Gee, Francesca. That's a mighty big word. You sure Ricky can handle your stellar vocabulary?'

Francesca hangs up.

And I smile.

The way I've smiled ever since Ben and I properly fell in love.

Today is the day I stop grinning and get busy. Time is up. My deadline is tomorrow. Delia is waiting for my first draft. No way am I going to let her down. So, with a pen and a notebook (in lieu of a laptop), I leave the Red Fox pub after my morning coffee and toast and head for the village square. It's too beautiful outside to work inside. I walk down the old cobblestone road and can't believe how bright the window box flowers are. Do we even have that shade of purple in New York? Is there a name for such a vivid red? Ahead, I see a bench beneath a tall, old tree that's the perfect inspiration for my piece.

I uncap my pen and begin.

Amazingly, my article practically writes itself. It's as if it's been silently lurking inside of me since I first set foot in London – growing, stretching, taking shape, bulking up. Like it's been there all along, but I didn't know it. Still, the weirdest thing happens: it's not until I write everything down that I realise exactly what I want to say.

I just hope it's what the editors at *Teen Scene* magazine want to hear.

TWENTY-FIVE

'Susanna!'

Delia greets me with another warm hug. I took the train in on my own this morning. Last night, Francesca told me she needed a break.

'I'm going to be a tourist,' she said. 'Ride the London Eye and all that.'

I burst out laughing. I guess Ricky's dad gave him another day off to take another American girl into the sky.

'What's so funny?' Francesca asked me.

'Nothing,' I said. 'I hear you can see Windsor Castle up there, but I doubt you will.'

Francesca gave me a snotty look. One of her specialities. I added, 'Just be sure to leave your cell on. In case I need to reach my supervisor.'

A little spiteful, I know. *Still*.

'Lovely to see you, Susanna,' Delia says. 'Have a seat in my office.'

Delia's office is nothing like Nell's. It's more of a comfortable living room than an icy snowdrift. I feel like I could slip off my shoes and curl up on her brown leather couch for a nap. Not that I ever would. But Nell's perfectly white couch never made me feel relaxed – just filled with terror that I'd start my period while sitting on it.

'How do you like London so far?' Delia asks me.

'I love it,' I say. 'It's gorgeous. Awesome. The perfect blend of old and new. It's—' I stop. 'Well, my impressions of your city are all in my article.'

Extending both hands, I offer up my latest attempt to further my budding career as a teen reporter. Hopefully, I give Delia proof that I'm more than a lucky kid who's in way over her head.

'Ah, yes,' she says. 'Your mighty opus.'

Thankfully, I took the time last night to input my handwritten article into Ashton's library computer. The printout looks professional and perfect. Still, all of a sudden, my heart pounds so strongly I'm sure Delia can feel the vibration across her desk.

'Let me take a look,' she says.

Delia puts on her reading glasses, takes my article and sits back in her desk chair. I sit forward in front of her.

'Chill out, Susanna,' she says. 'Have a coffee, if you like. I'll need a few minutes to read this.'

'Take your time,' I say. Then, totally unchilled-out, I sit and stare at her while she reads my first-ever international article.

It takes *forever*. Delia's eyes flick left and right as she reads each line. Her face is expressionless. Her lips tight. I scan her features for the briefest hint of approval – the crack of a smile, a knowing nod. I wait for her shoulders to shake as she chuckles. But there's nothing. Zippo. Soon, my shoulders *sag*. By the time Delia's gaze reaches the end of the first page, my chest feels like it's being squeezed between two closing elevator doors. Or, subway doors – the kind that don't open even if you're stuck in them.

'Hmmm,' Delia says, turning the page.

Hmmm? What does that mean? Hmmm, good? Hmmm, this is not at all what I wanted? Hmmm, why did we give this kid so much freedom?

My upper lip starts to sweat. I feel my heart pounding in my ears. Delia's face is still blank. Did she have Botox injections? I wonder. Is she excited, but I just can't tell?

'Ah,' she says.

Ah? If she said, 'Ooh,' I would be encouraged. Or

'Mmmm' instead of 'Hmmm'. Or if her thumb flickered in the tiniest upward motion. As it stands now, my international career is quickly sinking lower than a London Tube station.

'I can work on it,' I sputter. 'This is only a first draft.'

Delia nods and keeps reading. Expressionless.

Is the woman made of stone?

In one colossal crash, my confidence tumbles to the Persian rug beneath my feet. My neck is no longer able to hold my head upright. My chin nearly touches my chest. My eyes sting. What was I thinking? I'm a kid! A virgin! How could Nell ever have thought my take on the teen scene in London would be interesting enough to print in a magazine? I didn't even get an A on my Language Arts final last year. My teacher said my essay on the American ideal of beauty sounded too angry to be objective. Well, duh! Who wouldn't be mad if they went to Fashion Week and saw the genetic freaks that walk down the runway? I'm supposed to *want* to look like a lollipop with a humungous head and stick-like body? My hip bones should jut out further than my boobs? Claudia Schiffer's legs are the size of my arms and she's over thirty-five!

'That's it, then,' Delia says, finished reading at last.

She smiles as she carefully places my article on her desk. But I can't interpret it. It could be the grin of support, or the expression of pity.

'That's what?' I ask, chuckling. Pitifully.

Delia reaches for her phone and presses a button.

'Could you please send in the senior editors?'

A voice on the other end says, 'Straight away.'

Then Delia removes her reading glasses, and we are left to stare at each other.

'Like I said,' I say, 'it's only a first draft. Not even, really. It's more of a *pre*-first. I wrote it in one day, on a bench. Under a tree. I'm sure I could do better inside. At a desk. I can work on it here, if you like. In the office. Ashton is way too pretty. Not that it's ugly here.'

I bite the inside of my lip to keep myself from confessing I got a love bite on the London Eye when I should have been working.

Delia says, 'Relax, Susanna. A magazine is a collaborative effort.'

What does she mean by *that*? I swallow hard. We're all going to pitch in to rewrite my thoughts as an American teen in London? Together, are we going to face Nell Wickham in New York and tell her how badly I failed in London? Will we collaborate on my new future career? Do they know anyone at Starbucks? As soon as the editors file into Delia's office, it's painfully clear that I'm the only teen in the room. I'm the sole American, too, unless you count Delia who's probably an honorary Brit by now. Where's Francesca when you need her? Why, oh why, is my supervisor, my superior, my everything-above-me, such a slut?

'Before I express my opinion,' Delia says to the senior editors, 'I want Susanna to read her "American Teen in London" piece.'

'Aloud?' I ask, my lips smacking.

Delia just chuckles. Sure, now she smiles!

Handing me my article, she motions for me to stand up. Why does everything horrible happen when you're on your feet? I wonder. They don't even let guys sit down when facing a firing squad. Is that what I'm facing now? A firing squad? Every terror I've ever felt before an oral report comes flooding back to me. My chest is now compressed to the size of a peanut.

Still, I stand.

Get a grip, Susanna! I yell inside my head.

You're the Girl in the Trunk!

You walked the red carpet on Oscar Night!

Randall Sanders kissed your cheek!

You impressed Nell Wickham, flew across the Atlantic,

drank a beer, walked out on an older boy and fell in love with Ben!

'Urban Pirates: A Tale of Two Cities,' I read, aloud, my voice trembling. 'By Susanna Barringer, an American Teen in London.'

At least forty eyeballs stare at me. My cheeks feel like I just ran a summer marathon. I'd trade my airline ticket home for a glass of water. But there's no turning back now.

I unsuccessfully attempt a swallow, then begin.

'I flew to London with my stereotypes firmly in place,' I read. 'The countryside would be filled with Miss Marples, the city would be crawling with punks – their fingernails painted black, their eyeliner thick and smudged. A capital teeming with urban pirates. Nothing, of course, like my own city. New York City. The centre of the Universe. Where everyone and everything is cool.'

Someone snorts. I look up and see all those eyeballs staring at me. Freaking out, I quickly tilt my head back down and resume reading.

'I'll be leaving London, however, with a very different impression.'

Again, I try to swallow. But it's a no-go. Even my teeth feel dusty.

'First, in the interest of full disclosure,' I read, 'I confess that I am *not* one of the cool kids. I'd more likely cover the prom for the school paper than ever cover my head with the Prom Queen's tiara. In this city with a monarch, I'm definitely a commoner.'

A voice in the back of the room says, 'Duh.'

I don't look up. I barrel on.

'That said, here is one common teen's personal tale of two cities: New York and London. In New York, kids hang out at Dunkin' Donuts. In London, it's the pub. New York has Juicy Couture and shopping on Lower Broadway; London has Uttam and Camden Market. JLo sells her designs at Macy's; Kate Moss is the queen of Topshop. New York's Chelsea district is London's Soho; New York's SoHo is London's Chelsea. Jordin Sparks won *American Idol* while Leona Lewis won *X Factor*. There's Britney's meltdown versus Amy's rehab, *Star* magazine versus *Heat*, paparazzi hounding celebrities on both sides of the Atlantic. New York has Times Square while London's "circus" is Piccadilly. Kids who live outside of both cities wish they lived *in*. New York boys skateboard at the monument in Riverside Park, London boys roll around Westminster Abbey and the South Bank. After a long, cold winter, both sets of city-dwellers flock to the sunny side of the street. New Yorkers eat pizza and bagels, Londoners eat fish and chips and scones. Pasties are knishes. American coffee is English tea.'

The paper has stopped rattling in my hands. Which I'm beyond grateful for since it was the only sound in Delia's office. That and my dry lips unsticking themselves from my dusty teeth. Without looking up, I soldier on.

'I came to London looking for differences, but I've seen the opposite. To my amazement, we're more alike than not – in different ways, but similar nonetheless. I'm stunned to see that my tale of two cities has turned into one story of unity. Kids in both countries want the same things: to belong, to fit in ... or at least not be slammed for standing out. We want to hang with our friends, listen to music. We're dying to get out of school so we can get on with life.

'I've learned a deeper lesson, too. Television forms our images of the world. Movies and novels, too. What we don't see, we don't get. I never stopped to think that it wasn't real. Even 'reality' TV is totally unreal! How real can you be if you live in a fake house with cameras in every room? What genuine person defines love as multiple choice? Real kids have bad skin, good grades, and minds of our own. We're nerds and Goths and mathletes and athletes. Only one girl can be Prom Queen, the rest of us are commoners. We're flawed and unfashionable and longing to be otherwise. And size zero is as unreal as it gets.

'This reporter has been blind. It's taken three thousand miles to open my eyes. An international reality check. My new and improved vision is this: our planet only *feels* enormous. Disney was right . . . it's a *small* world after all. We're squished here together, desperate to hang on to our space, our nationality, our identity. But, what if we saw ourselves as citizens of the *universe*? Wouldn't we make room for everyone?

'After a month in London, that's what I'm bringing home. A new passport. And a plan: expand my vision beyond my borders. Stop thinking like an American; start thinking like a human. Care more about my planet, less about the stars in Hollywood. Accept my body shape, even though it's more like an 'O' than an 'I' and move over one tiny inch – two and a half centimetres – so even the Prom Queen has a place to stand.'

Exhaling loudly, I lower my paper, look up and say, 'Ta da.'

I crack a smile. But no one smiles back. The office is dead silent until that same voice in the back mutters, 'Did anyone bring a vomit bag?'

Everyone erupts in laughter. Even Delia. My face instantly turns pomegranate red.

Delia says, 'You're absolutely right, Miles. That article was so syrupy I may lapse into a diabetic coma.'

More laughter spurts out across the room.

'My first draft,' I squeak.

Miles mockingly sings, 'It's a small, small world.'

I want to crawl under the desk.

'Which is why I absolutely love it,' says Delia.

'I'll start my rewri— did you say you love it?' I ask.

'I adore it,' she says. 'All it needs is a tweak here and there.'

I've heard that word before. 'Tweak' is *publishese* for 'rewrite'. But I can handle that. I'm a professional. I'm the *Girl in the Tru*—

'Tweak?' Miles says, one eyebrow arched so high it practically hits his hairline. 'Is that our new word for the paper shredder?'

I wince. But Delia holds firm.

'We're so cynical,' she says. 'Why not publish a breath of fresh air?'

For the first time all morning, I take a full breath of fresh air. Miles exhales in a groan.

'C'mon, Delia. This piece is *so* Little Orphan Annie.' This time, he sings, 'The sun'll come out tomorrow.'

Delia says. 'What's wrong with that?'

'We need edge, antagonism, controversy,' Miles says. 'This is the first issue. We need to set a tone.'

The other editors nod enthusiastically.

'Exactly,' says Delia. 'What's edgier than optimism when the whole world is looking bleak? Why *not* look on the bright side?'

I grin. Brightly. Miles rolls his eyes.

Delia says, 'It's not a cover article. It's a short opinion piece. And I like to see opinions that aren't all negative. Don't you?'

Again, Miles dramatically rolls his eyes. Clearly, he likes it when the *clouds* come out. He's also the obvious leader of this group. No one else says a word. With me standing there, my article limp in my hands, and the other editors seated around the office, I watch Miles and Delia volley their opinions back and forth. Finally, Delia looks directly at me.

'Well done, Susanna,' she says. 'I knew I could count on you to give us something unique.'

Miles lowers his eyebrow and sighs.

I smile.

The way I've been smiling for days.

The way I plan to smile for the rest of my life.

TWENTY-SIX

The sun *does* come out tomorrow. And almost every day until it's time to go home. Delia's 'tweaks' are fairly painless. She asks me to be more inclusive of all kinds of kids.

'What about brainiacs? Class clowns? Cheerleaders?'

'I'm on it,' I say, spending the last few days in London making my article sing. Miles never likes it. And Francesca? Well, her reaction – you guessed it – is one long sneer. Not that I care. I figure she's just hungry.

On my last morning in Ashton, I don my enormous American Reeboks, comfy jeans and an Uttam shirt I bought at Camden Market. Then I use the last of my puny paycheck to buy a ticket on a tour bus for the one place I'm dying to see: Stonehenge. So I can see for myself.

On the way, I lean my head back and stare out the window. In the passing green fields, I see my future:

bright, fresh, green. I see nothing but possibility. School starts again next month, but I'm ready. I'll be entering my final years of high school with *life* experience. I, Susanna Barringer, have been there, done that. I'm a citizen of the *world*.

And I'm returning to a bona fide boyfriend.

'She made u *read* it?' Ben asked in his IM to me.

'Can u believe it?' I replied. 'I almost fainted!'

'But u didn't,' he wrote. 'U were awesome.'

That word – *awesome* – as in struck with awe, makes me feel, well, awesome. In the past year, so many dreams have come true. I never knew what I had inside of me until I dived into *life* to find out. I acted 'as if' until I began to believe myself.

After a long bumpy ride, the bus pulls into a parking lot across the road from Stonehenge. Once again, I can't believe I'm here. The sun is high up in the sky, and the enormous stones shine orange.

'Wow,' I say out loud, as I pass through a short tunnel beneath the road and emerge a few feet away from this ancient site.

'They are as old as the pyramids in Egypt,' a man behind me says.

He takes a photo with his phone, but I just take it all in with my eyes. Unlike the Statue of Liberty,

Stonehenge *doesn't* look smaller in person. It's gigantic. And impossible. This is one tourist hotspot that's truly worth the trip. A few of the humungous rectangular stones have fallen over, but most are upright. Some even have huge flat stones on top of them. The audio tour informs me that the 'small' bluestones in the inner circle were probably taken from mountains over two hundred miles away. Each stone weighs about four tons. The large stones in the outer circle weigh in at over *forty* tons and were probably transported from twenty miles away. As I walk on the grass all around the circular monument, I can't fathom how human beings could have done it. My arms get tired when I carry one of my little brothers a couple of blocks!

Maybe Stonehenge was built by aliens after all.

As I mull over the possible origins of Stonehenge, I think how weird it is that we'll never know who built it or why. Like Amelia Earhart. We'll never know for sure what happened to her plane. Or the Monarch butterflies. How do they know how to follow the exact same migration pattern year after year? Then I stop and look up at the amazing circle of rocks. That's when it hits me. It doesn't matter who built it or why. The only thing that matters is that they did it. Amelia was the first woman to fly solo coast to coast. The

Monarchs somehow figure out how to fly south every winter. That's what's important. *Doing* what you set out to do. Even when it's impossible.

'That's *so* "Little Orphan Annie",' I say out loud.

Then I laugh.

It's so *me*.

TWENTY-SEVEN

'Will you come back?' Blythe asks me at our farewell dinner in the pub.

'Some day,' I say, meaning it. 'Especially if you make these amazing sausages again.'

She laughs. Percy says, 'Blythe's bangers and mash are the best in England.'

Elbowing him in the ribs, Blythe says, 'What about Scotland and Wales?'

We're all grins. I toast my hosts with a diet soda. Even though I'm glad to be going home, I'm sad that my adventure is almost over. Nell's sister and her brother-in-law have been so nice to me, I hate to say goodbye. Oddly, it seems as if I've just arrived in Ashton *and* have lived there for years. Like I'm a tourist in my hometown.

'Maybe I'll take you to New York City one day,' Percy says to his wife.

Blythe winces. 'All those honking horns and crazy people!'

I laugh. 'Don't believe everything you see on TV.'

Francesca bustles into our goodbye dinner half an hour late.

'Sorry,' she says, flushed. 'The train was delayed.'

Nobody believes her. Not that anyone cares. If my time in England has taught me anything, it's that I'd rather be a Blythe than a Francesca. I'd rather have an inner package that's more beautiful than my outer one.

'Percy, will you make me a martini?' she says, dismissively.

What a jerk. Ricky can have her.

Since Francesca decided to spend a vacation week in London, I'm flying home on my own tomorrow. Which, really, is the icing on my trip. Knowing I won't have to see Francesca any time soon makes my inner package glow.

The ride to the airport is a reverse of my trip in. With Blythe at the wheel, we zoom past vast green fields and stone walls and small row houses with flower boxes in the windows.

Blythe says, 'Now you know why Nell fled Ashton.'

I nod. Nell, with her pointy shoes and narrow black skirts and platinum-blonde hair, would look like an extraterrestrial here. Was Nell ever one of those girls in the pub? Dying to get out, so she could get into life?

'But Nell will always have Ashton in her,' Blythe adds.

So will I, I think. London, too. How cool is that?

Blythe enters the airport at full speed, then lurches to a stop at the kerb in front of my terminal.

'I can't stand goodbyes,' she says. 'Though I won't mind booting your snotty boss out of my pub.'

I say, 'She's not my boss, my supervisor, my superior or anything above me any more!'

Climbing out of her old banger, Blythe circles the car and gives me a big hug. I hug her back and thank her for everything. Suddenly, I feel tears pool in my eyes.

'None of that,' Blythe says.

When she pulls away, I see that her eyes are misty, too. Mel is right. Goodbyes should be instantaneous; hellos should be drawn out.

'I'm off,' I say, sniffling.

'Tell my sister to eat something, will you?'

We laugh. Blythe gets back in her car, toots the horn, and takes off. I wave, but she doesn't look back.

So, making sure my passport is handy, I roll my suitcase into the airport.

The clock is ticking.

It's time to go home.

TWENTY-EIGHT

The flight to New York is surreal. Instead of losing hours with the time difference, I gain them. My plane leaves Heathrow at 6:30 in the evening, I fly for eight hours, then land in New York at 9:30 that same night. How weird is that?

In flight, I stare out the window the same way I did on the bus to Stonehenge. Instead of green fields, I see darkening blue skies. Clouds instead of sheep. I try to reflect on the past few weeks – how I've changed – but my eyelids soon droop. My brain fuzzes up. Before I even realise it, I'm asleep. Dreaming of a boy named Ashton who looks exactly like Ben.

'Ladies and gentlemen, we're beginning our descent into John F. Kennedy Airport,' the flight attendant says over the intercom.

I awake with a jerk of my head.

'We're home?' I say, groggy.

Impossibly, I slept the whole way.

'Please make sure your seatbelt is securely fastened,' the flight attendant continues, 'and your seat backs are in their locked, upright position.'

The American woman next to me scoffs.

'Do they really think that flimsy strap will protect us?' she says.

I flash on the British man who was next to me on the plane a month ago when I flew the other way. He said the exact same thing! I chuckle. It's really true – we *are* all the same. Only in slightly different ways.

'We'll be landing in a few minutes,' the flight attendant says. 'Enjoy your stay in New York. Have a nice evening.'

Several minutes later, we touch down with a bump and a skid. The plane taxis so long it feels like the airline is driving us home. When we finally reach the gate, I can't wait to get off the plane and set foot in my city. When I do, the first thing I do is inhale. I smell the air conditioning of JFK, the warm icing of a nearby Cinnabon. Freshly-ground Starbucks coffee.

The aroma of home.

Though I've flown all night, I feel totally awake. There's a long line to show our passports, and another line to get through customs, but I don't care. I know what's waiting for me at the end of it.

'Susanna?'

Before I see his face, I spot the giant bouquet. Sunflowers. My favourite. Fresh and big and bright.

Right there in the airport, I burst into tears.

'Ben!'

I fling my arms around him. Kiss him all over his face. Ben looks startled. I can tell he's nervous. His hair is over-gelled. His T-shirt looks ironed. My heart melts. Taking the flowers I blubber, 'These are *almost* as beautiful as you.'

Ben grins. It's not lopsided like Ricky's. His hair isn't all punked out in spikes. He's not older or exotic. His accent doesn't make him sound more intelligent than he is. Ben is just *Ben*.

The boy who has my heart.

My love.

The *one*.

TWENTY-NINE

'Traffic is jammed on the Van Wyck,' our cab driver says.

'How 'bout the Belt Parkway?' Ben asks.

'Better than the tunnel.'

I smile. Guys talking traffic. Nothing has changed.

Our cab driver loops around lower Manhattan, past the Verrazano Bridge, along New York Harbour. The Statue of Liberty's torch flickers like a giant firefly in the night sky. The Hudson shimmers like a huge slab of black granite.

Ben and I hold hands in the back seat.

He says, 'I've missed you.'

'I've missed you more.'

'Yeah, right.'

I slide over as far as my seatbelt will let me. I want to confess that I've been an idiot. That I needed to get away so I could become close. That I was blind until the London Eye gave me sight. It's all in my heart, but I can't get words past my lips.

'It's okay,' Ben whispers.

He looks incredibly vulnerable. For a second, it looks like he might cry. Which makes me want to cry. Then I remember that look in his eyes. It's intensity, not tears. Ben loosens his seatbelt and slides over to me. We gaze at each other in silence for a full minute. Then, I reach out and take his face in my hands. I pull his lips to mine. Press. Kiss. It's a perfect fit. My palms are warm, his cheeks are hot. Our two hearts are audible. The sound of true love.

Ben's lips are so soft, I barely feel them at first. I taste the minty gum he was chewing. Smell his Chapstick. I push harder, he pushes back. Our kiss is full of unspoken words. The promise of our future. It feels completely familiar and absolutely new. I don't want the cab ride to end. If we could loop around Manhattan until we ran out of gas, my homecoming would be complete.

'Hungry?' Ben says, softly.

I laugh. We both heard my stomach growl.

'Always,' I say.

He leans forward and asks the cab driver to drop us off at the corner of Bleeker and Sixth Avenue in lower Manhattan. I pull my cell out of my handbag and call my parents.

'You're here!' Mom squeals.

'Ben and I are going to grab something to eat.'

Mom sighs. 'I guess I can't expect you to want to rush home to your old *mum*,' she says.

'Sorry, Mum!' I reply in my best British accent. 'I'll be home straight away.'

My mom laughs. 'Don't be silly. Have fun.'

'Are the Trips asleep?'

'Yeah.'

'Dad on a case?'

'Yeah.'

I pause. Stunned by how normal everything sounds.

Mom says, 'I'll see you at home tonight.'

'I love you, Mom.'

'Ditto.'

The cab driver lets us off steps away from one my favourite spots in the world: John's Pizzeria. The best pizza in New York. Ben pays the fare and the tip and grabs my suitcase. I fill my arms with sunflowers.

Initially, it's a shock to stand on the street. It's after eleven and people are all over the place. Boys in baggy shorts play basketball in the lit court on the corner. A group of kids listens to music in front of Dunkin' Donuts. A bus passes, filled with passengers. Then I catch myself. This is New York. The city that never sleeps. Where people eat pizza all day and night.

Ben orders a pepperoni pizza and two Cokes.

'Diet Coke for me, please,' I say. I am, after all, back in the land of size zero. Not that I'll ever get *there*. Or even close. Or even want to now that Naomi Campbell has proven how spitting mad you can get when you're starving.

Ben heads for the restroom while I sit at our table and pull a mirror out of my handbag. As usual, my curls are a mess – too flat on one side, too full on the other. My lips are pale and dry. My eyes bloodshot. Still, I see something beautiful in my reflection. Something surprising. I look *different*. It takes a few moments for me to realise what it is.

I look grown-up.

Not *fully* grown, of course. I still have a long way to go. But, as I wait for the best pizza and the best boyfriend, I see that it's happened: I've tiptoed over the edge of my childhood into the beginning of my adulthood. It took six thousand miles – to England and back – for me to get there. But here I am.

'No pizza yet?' Ben returns and swings his skinny frame into the seat across from mine.

'Not yet,' I say.

He takes my hand across the table.

'Jason and I finished our online video last night,' he says.

My eyes light up. 'Really?'

'We're going to post it on YouTube tomorrow.'

'Awesome!'

Our pizza arrives and fills the air with a smoky, cheesy smell. My tastebuds explode with joy the moment I take a bite. The crust is perfectly thin and crunchy, the pepperoni is spicy, the tomato sauce has just the right kick. I shut my eyes and sigh. Nothing tastes more like home than John's.

'Thirty thousand a year for international students.'

My eyes fly open and I can't believe who I see.

'Amelia!' Leaping to my feet, I drop my slice on my plate and fling my arms around my best friend.

'Oxford may be the best deal of all,' she says. 'So, if you go back to England, I may go with you.'

I hug her again. 'How did you know I was here?'

'Ben called me.'

Ben grins with his greasy lips. It takes all my willpower to keep from flying across the table to kiss him. While I thought he was in the bathroom, he was calling Amelia? How cool is that?

Mel sits, grabs a slice of pizza and a napkin and says, 'I'm thinking maybe a law degree.'

Ben asks, 'If you study law at Oxford, do you have to wear those funny wigs to class?'

'Will you call yourself a *solicitor*?' I ask, sliding into the booth with my two friends.

We can't stop grinning. Together, in John's, we sit and eat pizza. It feels so *normal*. Ben touches my foot under the table. He strokes the back of my calf with the front of his trainer. Our gazes lock and he smiles with his eyes. How could I ever have thought I'd find someone better than Ben? I feel my heart expand to fill my entire chest.

'I don't want you to go to USC,' I say to him.

He says, 'I hope you don't go back to England.'

Mel asks, 'How far is Oxford from London?'

'Too far,' I reply.

We chew in silence. I feel the oil from the pepperoni spread over the roof of my mouth, hear the crunch of the crust. I think about Blythe and Percy and Ashton. I flash on the London Eye, Ricky's hair, Francesca's sneer. I can almost smell the horses in the English countryside and the sausages in Borough Market. I feel the heavy grey mist of a London morning, hear the *chuga-chug*, *chuga-chug* of the train. I want to share it all with my best friend and my boyfriend.

But not now.

'Who's up for bagels tomorrow?' I ask.

Ben nods. 'Zabar's?'

'We can eat in the park,' Mel adds.

'I'll bring Starbucks,' I say.

Outside, a horn honks. Tyres screech. Someone yells, 'Get out of the road, you old hag!'

Somebody else yells, 'Hey! That's somebody's mother!'

'Oh yeah? My mistake. Get out of the road, you *mother*!'

I shake my head and smile. Then I feel a strange sensation. Time stops still for a nanosecond. The molecules in the air around me freeze. It's as if there's a snapshot of my life. Right here, right now. This moment. It's complete. Bliss. Nirvana. There is nowhere else I'd rather be. No *one* else I'd rather be . . . or be with. Me. My peeps. My body. My city. This table. That pizza.

It's perfect.

I, Susanna Barringer, celebrity reporter *extra-ordinaire*, opinion columnist, breath of fresh air, Girl in the Trunk, walker on the red carpet, curves in the fashion closet, Nell's intern, Francesca's outcast,

Ricky's reality girl, Ben's proper GF, Mel's forever BFF, and citizen of the entire planet, am *home*.

'Share the last slice?' Ben asks.

I wouldn't have it any other way.

IF YOU ENJOYED
SUSANNA LOVES LONDON,
LOOK OUT FOR THE
NEXT NOVEL BY

MARY HOGAN

PERFECT GIRL,
COMING SOON!

HERE'S A TASTER ...

ONE

She walks into class ten minutes after the bell. Twenty heads turn. Forty eyes watch her walk up to the front with her perfectly tanned legs, perfectly blue halter-neck top and perfectly sweeping fringe.

Mr Roland is already boring us. Chalk dust flying, he lists the six member councils of the United Nations on the board. His short-sleeved white shirt is so thin you can see the shadow of his back hair.

'... General Assembly, Security Council ...' his nasal voice drones on.

'I'd like to member her council,' one of the guys says, flicking his head at the new girl. The class erupts in laughter. Well, the *boys,* anyway.

'Oh my,' Mr Roland says, turning around. 'Who do we have here?'

She hands him a note. I stare and twirl a strand of red hair around my finger.

'Take a seat,' our teacher says. And the new girl

does. She calmly walks to the back of the room without blushing, though everyone is watching her every move. Especially Marcus. *My* Marcus.

'This is Jenna Wilson, everyone,' says Mr Roland. The boys nod and smirk. The girls curl their lips up in fake smiles. Jenna sits and faces the front. I notice she has a French manicure on her fingers and her toes. Curling my ragged nails into my palms, I face the front too.

'... Economic and Social Council, International Court of Justice ...'

Mr Roland returns to the chalkboard and blathers on. The way he has all term. I hear with my ears, but my mind is on the new girl. The *perfect* girl, who now sits between me and Marcus Gould. I feel him checking her out. My heart sinks.

Of all times, why *now*?

TWO

'Duck.'

That's the first word I ever heard him say. The one I remember, anyway. It came flying over the chain-link fence that separates our two backyards. He might have been identifying the airborn rubber duck, or telling me to get out of the way. Who knows? What I *do* know is this: from day one, Marcus Gould and I have been friends. *Best* friends, probably. But don't tell my other best friend, Celeste.

Marcus still lives on Fifth Street in Odessa, Delaware; I still live on Sixth. We've been connected all our lives by geography. Now, I'm hoping for some anatomical connection, too.

'Duck,' I'd repeated as a little kid, tottering over to retrieve the yellow rubber bird in my backyard.

Marcus's mom sunned herself on a deckchair beside their paddling pool. My mother was on her hands and knees, planting herbs in our vegetable garden.

Mrs Gould shouted, 'Sorry!' Then she asked, 'Want to come swimming, Ruthie?'

Of course I did. But, Mom's forehead got all creased with thoughts of bacteria, drowning—

'I won't take my eyes off her, Fay,' said Mrs Gould.

Reluctantly, Mom let me go next door.

'I'll get her bathing suit and the sunscreen,' she said, grunting as she got up.

By the time she returned, however, I was through the gate, stripped down to my underpants, and splashing Marcus in his pool. That was our first date. Marcus saw me topless when being topless didn't mean a thing. We played together long before life complicated every touch.

'What do you think Jenna stands for?' Celeste asks me after social studies class. 'Jennifer?'

'Wouldn't that be Jenn*i* instead of Jenn*a*?' my second-best friend, Frankie, asks. Her real name is Frances, which actually suits her better since she's shy and round and a bit of a follower. Unlike Celeste, who charges forward into every situation not caring who she ploughs over.

Celeste won't admit it, but she's a bit of a Frances

inside. And I see myself in both of them. Probably the reason we all get along. Most of the time.

I say, 'Maybe she spells it *Jennafer*, with an "a".'

Celeste says, 'God, I hope not.'

'Me, too,' I say. 'How naff can you get?'

'Yeah,' echoes Frankie. 'How naff can you get?'

We silently walk across the grass to our lunch spot. I hurry to get in the shade. The last thing I need is another freckle. My long red hair is already frizzing in the afternoon humidity. Celeste plops down in the direct sun, twists her straight black hair into a knot, and tilts her face skywards. Frankie rolls her tight capri pants up over her knees and kicks off her flip-flops. I notice that she forgot to rub self-tanning cream on the tops of her feet.

As we open our packed lunches, I know my friends are thinking what I'm thinking. Isn't freshman year hard enough without a new girl? A *perfect* girl?

'Besides,' Celeste says, her eyes closed, 'who comes to a new school right at the end of the year?'

'Yeah,' says Frankie. 'Who?'

'Maybe her parents are fugitives,' I suggest.

'Delaware's Most Wanted,' Celeste says, laughing.

Frankie asks, 'Do you think their pictures are on-line?'

There she is across the lawn. She's heading straight for us. Her long, light-brown hair flips right and left with each step. Her thigh muscles flex as she walks down the hill. Already, she's been swallowed up by the Semi-Populars. Two girls from the soccer team are showing her around. My pulse races as they get close, but they pass our tree without acknowledging us at all. Not that we look like we care. Celeste glances at her, then closes her eyes again. Frankie takes a bite of her peanut butter sandwich. Me, I flip my hair and pretend I don't notice her deep dimples or the way her eyes crinkle when she laughs. *At least she's not blonde,* I think. Thank God for small favours.

'Hey.'

My heart flutters as I hear a familiar voice behind me.

'Hey, Marcus,' I say, flipping my hair again and turning around. Marcus nods at me but I see his eyes shift to *her*. To my horror, she looks right at him and smiles. Crud. Now he's seen her deep dimples, too.

I squint and look up at the boy I'm inexplicably ga-ga over. The only boy who's seen me topless and knows all my secrets. Marcus bobs his head to the hip-hop music in his ears. He wears a gigantic white T-shirt over huge, hem-frayed jeans. Celeste opens one eye and scoffs. Admittedly, his outfit *is* a tad lame. Especially the woolly hat when it's, like, ninety degrees out. But Marcus will try anything not to look like the science nerd he is – even fronting like a gangster.

'You're not fooling anyone,' I've told him a million times. Marcus even looks clever eating cornflakes in the morning. He's going to be an astronaut. The astronomy class at Liberty High was created for him and the other brains who are so far beyond ninth grade science it's not even funny. Marcus's idea of the perfect vacation is a shuttle flight to the Space Station. I mean, come *on*.

At school, though, Marcus pretends he's a boy from the 'hood without a stratospheric gross point average. I used to think he was out of his mind. Now, when I look at him, I feel like I'm going out of mine.

'We're *busy*,' Celeste says to Marcus, all snotty. 'Try not to trip on your pants when you leave, Bozo.'

'Try not to confuse your age with your IQ,' Marcus says to Celeste, nodding at me again, then pimp-walking away.

'Later!' I say to Marcus, wincing at how desperate I sound. Annoyed, I ask Celeste, 'Why do you have to be so mean to him?'

'He's mean to *me*.'

'You were mean first.'

'What, are we in kindergarten? Who cares about Marcus? It's not like he's your boyfriend, Ruthie,' Celeste says. 'It's not like I *have* to like him.'

I swallow. 'He *is* my friend.'

'Your *sympathy* friend. Just because you were friends as kids doesn't mean you need to be friends now.'

What could I say? I didn't have the guts to tell my best friend that I was officially in love with Marcus Gould. She can't see into his poet's soul the way I suddenly can. And if I told Frankie about my new thing for Marcus, she'd instantly blab to Celeste. Which is why Frankie will always be best friend number *two*.

Most of all, neither one of my friends would understand what happened last Friday night. Particularly since I don't understand it myself.

THREE

It was deliciously warm out, one of those pre-summer nights that makes you crazy because school is almost over, but finals are still ahead. It's like you're dying to be free but you can't let go. Not yet.

'Check this out,' Marcus said.

We were up on the flat part of his roof – like we always were – hanging out. Marcus was staring at the stars through the monster telescope his mother saved for two years to buy him. It was tilted towards the black sky, standing on its tripod. Me, I was thinking about how your whole life can be formed by an accident. Not in the 'car wreck' sense. In the 'not on purpose' sense. Like, where you live. And the fact that a totally abnormal life has to be *your* life because that's all you were given.

'Ruthie, check this out,' Marcus repeated.

'It better be good,' I said. Stars, to me, are a waste of

time. Unless, of course, we're talking about Orlando Bloom.

Crouching down, I pressed the eyepiece up to my face.

'See it?' Marcus asked, excited.

'I see a white dot.'

'That's it!' He stepped closer to me. 'Vega! It's the brightest star in the Summer Triangle.'

I looked, then shrugged.

'Can you see Epsilon Lyrae right next to it?' he asked. 'Can you?'

What, I was looking for *two* dots now? Pulling my eye away from the telescope, I asked Marcus, 'Do you ever wonder how totally different you'd be if you lived in Alaska or California or New York?'

'It's a *double* star, Ruthie,' he said. 'You can't always see it.'

'That's what I'm saying! How can you see who you really are when you're stuck in someone else's life?'

Marcus rolled his eyes. We'd had this discussion before.

The two of us were trapped in a maternal noose. Both only children. Both dadless. Marcus's father ran off with a shiatsu massage therapist from Dover when he was two. My dad . . . well, he never *was*. Mom chose me the way you pick sheets.

'I'd like green ones to match the bedspread. Make sure they're the right size because they have to fit what I already have.'

My mother selected my red hair and blue eyes to match her own. She chose a dad who was in college, because she never went. I had a little heart disease in my paternal genes, she told me, but no more than the average person.

Average person. How could I ever be average when my father was only a sperm in a syringe?

'No child was wanted more than you,' Mom said. It took two expensive tries at the fertility clinic in Wilmington for me to take. 'Why else would I go to so much trouble?'

My mom has lived in tiny Odessa, Delaware, all her life. Population: two hundred and eighty-six. Before I was born (Population: two hundred and eighty-*five),* my mom worked at the only diner in town.

'I knew everyone,' she told me. 'No one was interested in me.'

My question is this: if Mom had waited, would a stranger have stopped by Taylor's Diner – someone who hadn't known her all his life, like Marcus had known me – and decided she was *the one*? Was a normal dad only a breakfast special away?

Marcus feels it, too. That *fizzing*. Like club soda in your veins. A constant reminder that you're not like everybody else. Not enough to take over your whole life, but enough to nag at you and keep *normal* just out of reach.

I'm not naive. I know nobody is completely normal. Even when people look and act normal, they aren't normal deep down. But they probably have a moment when they *feel* normal. When they buy a Father's Day card without thinking twice about it, when their dads teach them how to drive, or walk them down the aisle. They have family stories and photos and Christmas mornings that are littered with torn wrapping paper. They don't feel like their mothers would shrivel up and die without them.

It's those little moments that add up to a family. When your dad isn't around, you don't know exactly what you're missing. You just know it's something big.

Most of the time, I stop my mind from dwelling on it. Because when I do, I stress out. Did my mother ever *once* consider what her decision might mean to me? Did it occur to her that a girl needs a dad so she can grow up to understand boys?

'If you look carefully, Ruthie, you'll see something truly amazing,' Marcus said last Friday night on top of his roof. 'The two stars of Epsilon Lyrae are actually *double* stars as well.'

Peering through the telescope, I could feel his breath on the back on my neck, his warm hand on my shoulder.

'So Epsilon is a double-double star. Can you see it? Can you see all four of them? They're awesome. You've got to see them.'

I stared until four dots came into focus. 'Oh.'

'You see them?'

Marcus's forehead pressed lightly against the back of my head. It felt totally familiar, but somehow, completely new.

Yeah, I saw them.

'Aren't they awesome?' he asked.

'They are.' For the first time, I meant it.

'Do you realize you're looking at massive nuclear reactions held together by gravitational force?'

I hadn't.

'*Astronaut* means *space sailor*,' he said, almost

dreamily. 'That's what I want to be – a space sailor.'

We both fell silent, imagining Marcus sailing into space, seeing Earth as a beach ball, feeling like a small dot.

I pulled away from the telescope, slightly dizzy. Then I gazed at Marcus's face. It was like I'd never truly seen him before. I could hardly catch my breath. His jaw was angular. His brown freckles had faded. Had his eyelashes always been long and curly? He had sideburns, sort of. And one crooked tooth. Why had I ever thought it looked goofy? And was he always so *tall*? All of a sudden, I noticed that Marcus had grown into his face and body. They weren't overtaking him anymore. He looked . . . *cute*. It took all my energy to keep from reaching my hand up to make sure he was real.

That's when it happened. *Thwang*. It was the steam coming off his chest, his grasslike smell, the feeling that we were all alone – just the two of us – on a tiny patch of roof in the middle of an infinite universe. Just us fatherless space sailors held together by gravitational force. As unexpected as a shooting star, that was the moment I fell in love with my (almost) best friend.

'Some nights you can see the Ring Nebula,' Marcus said. 'But not now. It's too early.'

He was wrong. It was too *late*. I was weightless in his orbit. I would never view Marcus Gould as my 'pal' again. It was beyond my control. My heart knew it, my knees knew it. If only I could figure out a way to let Marcus in on the news.

Before someone – like the new girl, the *perfect* girl – gets her French-manicured hands on my soon-to-be (*please* God!) boyfriend.

PERFECT GIRL BY MARY HOGAN – COMING SOON!

ACKNOWLEDGEMENTS

Quite simply, this book would have been impossible without my brilliant editor, Venetia Gosling, who guided me (and Susanna) with skill and heart. Endless thanks to Ingrid Selberg and her awesome staff at S&S UK, especially publicists Rachel Williams and Sheelagh Cullinan who cheerfully *schlepped* me (an American term!) all over England. Thank you, as well, to my UK agent, Annette Green, and the phenomenal Laura Langlie, my US literary agent and friend. Finally, for being the best support system and travelling companion a girl could ever have, my husband and the love of my life, Bob.